MY TRAITOR

4 mai 2011

MY TRAITOR

Sorj Chalandon

Sorj Chalandon

THE LILLIPUT PRESS
DUBLIN

First published 2007 by Éditions Grasset & Fasquelle, Paris

Published in 2011 by
THE LILLIPUT PRESS
62–63 Sitric Road, Arbour Hill
Dublin 7, Ireland
www.lilliputpress.ie

Translated from the French by Fiona McCann and Kitty Lyddon

Copyright © Sorj Chalandon, 2011

ISBN 978 1 84351 183 0

1 3 5 7 9 10 8 6 4 2

All rights reserved. No part of this publication may
be reproduced in any form or by any means
without the prior permission of the publisher.

A CIP record for this title is available
from The British Library.

Set in 12 pt on 16 pt Perpetua by Marsha Swan
Printed in Scotland by Thomson Litho of Glasgow

CONTENTS

Tyrone Meehan	13
James Connolly	25
A Terrible Beauty	37
Mise Éire	53
Interrogation of Tyrone Meehan by the IRA	
16 DECEMBER 2006	69
The Martyr	73
A Coffin on My Shoulder	86
The Ceasefire	97
Interrogation of Tyrone Meehan by the IRA	
17 DECEMBER 2006	101
My Traitor	105
Interrogation of Tyrone Meehan by the IRA	
18 DECEMBER 2006	115
The Secret	119
The Silence	130
Interrogation of Tyrone Meehan by the IRA	
20 DECEMBER 2006	144
Gypo Nolan	147
Gráinne O'Doyle	156
Afterword: Why *My Traitor*?	173

For Aude

MY TRAITOR

I am standing on the threshold of another trembling world.
May God have mercy on my soul.

> *Bobby Sands, Irish patriot, March 1981,*
> *on the first day of his hunger strike.*

"A WORD to BE caught & ceremoniously woven".

to Spell Bind.

TYRONE MEEHAN

The first time I saw my traitor, he taught me how to take a piss. It was in Belfast, in the Thomas Ashe, a club reserved for ex Republican prisoners. I was near the door, beside the large fireplace, sitting at a table covered with empty glasses and dead bottles. It was the favourite spot of Jim and Cathy O'Leary, who offered me a bed whenever I came to Northern Ireland. Jim O'Leary was a friend. He had done time for transporting arms. He was a joiner, but Catholic, and therefore unemployed, like his wife. And he remained unemployed until the end.

The first time I saw my traitor was that evening, 9 April 1977, in the company of Cathy and Jim O'Leary. Jim was coming back from the bar, three pints of beer held tightly in his big hands. A dark, bitter beer, as heavy as a winter meal, with a sweetish ochre head that turned your stomach. He put the drinks down in front of me. He was joking with a man at a nearby table. In the Thomas Ashe, Jim knew everyone. The small crowd, living between freedom and captivity, was at home around these beer-filled tables; they had their own way of life behind the barbed wire. That Easter Saturday, I had been drinking since the middle of the afternoon. One pint here, another there, waiting for Jim to finish his business. He had brought me to the Rock, to the Busy Bee, another place protected by a doorman, a detour round a dead end, a meeting in a park, a handshake with Father Mullan, three words murmured in Irish to a passer-by, a banknote slipped into a hand, an intrigue between two doors. And I followed Jim. I was privy to no secret, no confidences. I barely paid attention. I never asked any questions. I was just proud to be walking with him along the worried streets, where these people greeted him. I was proud because they noticed me at his side. They remembered my face, and Antoine, my name.

It was early evening. The beers kept coming and coming. My eyes were stinging from the cigarettes. I was drunk. From all the pints. Jim's laugh and the laughter all around. The rough exclamations, the tumultuous waves that shook the tables. The look on Cathy's face as she searched for her reflection in a raised glass. And then that music.

—A rebel song, Jim whispered to me.

I looked over towards the stage.

O then tell me, Sean O'Farrell, where the gath'rin' is to be?

I remember closing my eyes. I had my pint in my hand, and two others waiting on the wet table.

The musicians were singing of the war.

When I first came to Ireland, I had little knowledge of the language of this country. When it was the rough, country, stony accent of Kerry, or the earthy Donegal accent, I did not understand a thing. I let the English words probe my school memory. I caught a sentence, a sound, not much. The musicians were singing of the war. A rebel song, Jim had said. But what about? I didn't know. It was over my head. I simply listened to the pain of the violin and the plaintive notes. For a long time, all I remembered of the Irish words was their harmony, their colour, their effect on the people sitting at the tables around me. Later, a long time after, hearing them over and over again, I was able to make sense of these lamentations. Those that mourned the Great Famine, those that celebrated the 1916 Rising, those that told of the War of Independence, or the hunger-strike martyrs. But when I first started coming to Ireland, I would just let myself get carried away by the seriousness of the people. I watched them covertly. I let myself be guided by a woman's raised hand, or by a man standing facing the stage, saluting the song like an old soldier. I nodded my head along with them. I held my fist in the air when they did. I laughed when they laughed and stood when they stood. Often, between two songs, a musician would talk into a mike. It was as brief as a salute. A few words, a name I understood because it was uttered with respect. Then the singer would point his finger towards a table at the back of the room and a man would stand up, half-laughing, half-shy, applauded by the standing crowd.

—He did thirteen years. He was released this morning, Jim might whisper.

Or else it was a prisoner's wife, applauded as a guest because she came from another town. Or the mother of an IRA volunteer, killed in action, who was remembered. Or else it was an American visitor with Irish roots, huddled in a new Aran jumper, wavering in the face of all this attention.

One thing and one thing only was instantly familiar to me: the Irish national anthem. 'A Soldier's Song' was my first landmark. Sometimes it would be played at the beginning of the evening when you gently set your pint on the table, still thinking about the day just past. Other times, the band would play it at the end of the evening, to let you know it was closing time, just before the lights were switched off and then back on again in the most violent way, with glass collectors shouting that it was time to go home. I have always loved that moment when the anthem is played. That communion, that ceremony of belonging, when Ireland calls her daughters and her sons to the foot of the flag. Jim no longer had to tell me when it was time. Even before it was played, in the silence after the songs, the way in which the musicians got themselves into a new position on the stage, in the solemn waiting, the anthem had already begun. And there, in the midst of everyone, standing amongst them all, with the same look of pain, the same chalk-white face, the same rain-drenched hair, the same feeble breathing, I was just like an Irishman.

∼

On that Saturday, 9 April 1977, I arrived in the morning, for a few days, as usual. I had left France, Paris, the neighbourhood around Place de l'Europe, my little workshop, the smell of wood and varnish, all that unsmiling grey, to come here and close my eyes.

—This is your home, Jim said.

It wasn't true yet, not quite. I had only been coming regularly to Northern Ireland for two years and I still had a guest's habits. I amused them. I would push a bar door instead of pulling it; I looked left before crossing the road; I would wait for my beer to be finished before ordering another. But even so. Here I was, once again, among them. I was the Frenchman at Cathy and Jim's table. I was just there, because it was normal, because people greeted me on the streets, because cars from the neighbourhood beeped their horns at me, because I came here without asking for anything, without demanding anything, without explaining anything and without taking anything. On the Falls Road, in Divis Flats, in Whiterock, in Ballymurphy, in the Short Strand, in Springfield, in Ardoyne, in the Markets, in Andytown, in these areas of extreme poverty, of ugly beauty and of violence that newspapers fear, Belfast whispered to me that I was, in some way, at home.

I wasn't the only foreigner roaming these streets. Journalists wandered everywhere, as well as sympathizers for the Republican cause: Germans, English, Dutch, French who talked too loudly, Americans overwhelmed by their ancestors. They walked around these places of Republican combat, without ever being able to enter them. When they pushed open a pub door, conversations died out. Not maliciously, not aggressively. They just died out, that's all. Wariness and old habits made the locals stop. But when I pushed open the club door and sat at Jim's table, the voices had other things on their mind. I was the violin-maker from Paris, the silent one, the one who came here to share some time.

∼

The first time I saw my traitor was that day, in that club, on Easter Saturday. I was standing, fists clenched by my sides because the musicians were playing my anthem. My head was spinning. Eyes closed, enveloped in the smell of turf. 'A Soldier's Song' was in full swing. On the last note, the room clapped. Not in a congratulatory way, but in thanks. I felt good, sitting back down at the table beside the door. Jim was still standing, putting his coat on, but was having difficulty with the sleeves. Cathy was huddled in conversation with a woman with her back to me. I needed to take a piss.

The toilets were in the basement, beyond the bar stocks and the piled-up kegs. A dozen or so men were there, talking about anything and everything. There were hands gripping shoulders, loud voices, drunken promises, tired eyes; zips open, even before reaching the urinal. There was unity, roughness, laughter, hoarse voices, battered faces, hair greasy with cigarette smoke, weary looks. And me, pissing with my forehead pressed against the tiles. Clumsily shielding myself and the quiet splatter of urine.

—Watch your shoes, son, my traitor said, smiling.

I looked at him. Piercing blue eyes, bushy eyebrows, white hairs creating chaos above his ears. He was unshaven. Under the neon lights, a worn face speckled with silver. Beside me. Pissing like me. A cigarette butt in the corner of his mouth, with one eye almost closed. Pissing like me, but he was farther away, with something almost elegant about his stance. In fact, *he* was elegant. A small man, in a brown tweed jacket with ochre and green thread, a checked shirt and dark woollen tie. He had kept his cap on. A brown herringbone cap from Shandon's, pure wool, soft from good use. A lot later, years after, he and I went to Donegal together, beyond Lough Foyle, in the Republic, just to buy me the same one.

—Do you want me to show you?

I still had the anthem in my head, beers to drink, Jim and Cathy who were waiting. All those sounds from the back of the room that sang of drunkenness. I too was out of it.

—Do you want me to show you? my traitor said again.

—Show me what?

—How to take a piss.

So I said yes.

I was facing the urinal – a spout, a gutter that ran along the wall. My traitor placed one hand on my shoulder and gently pulled me back. I was still pissing. It was hanging out. I hadn't had time to put it away. He laughed. Not nastily. He was just amused at my embarrassment. He asked me what the hell I was afraid of. That someone would see my penis? Here? In this men's room? This prisoners' bar?

Come on! Smiling, he pointed at my shoes. I was so close to the wall, so worried about it all, the urine was hitting off the white tiles and splashing back onto my shoes in small embarrassing drops.

—That's not how you do it, he told me.

Standing, facing the urinal, he took three steps back and placed his left hand against the wall.

—It's like this.

He was stable. Feet spread out, one hand above his head, flat on the tiles, and the other directing the flow. He stood there, like that, stretched out like a bridge, bracing himself above the urinal. He looked at me. There, he said, like this. Once the body was positioned like that, away from the communal gutter, a man could let himself go. I was still standing back, urine on my shoes.

He pissed for a long time.

I had noticed him before, earlier that evening. He was at a big table near the stage. A table of men whom everyone greeted. I saw him because he was looking at me. He talked as he watched me. He laughed as he watched me. He raised his glass as he watched me. When it was time for the national anthem, he had stood up. When I opened my eyes on the last note, he was putting his cap back on. And now here he was pissing. Showing me how. One arm stretched out, a balanced body, and no splashes anywhere.

—You French?

I looked at my traitor. My zip was still down. He let me know with a flick of his chin. We went out together, returning to the over-lit bar.

—I could spot you a mile off. The French move their upper lip when they talk, said my traitor.

I smiled, not knowing what else to do.

—Where do you live?

—Paris.

—Have you got a job?

—I'm a violin-maker.

Sideways look from my traitor.

—Violence-maker?

—Violin-maker.

—Oh! A violin-maker? You're young.

—Thirty-two.

He nodded, buttoning up his jacket. All around, women and men were struggling to get up. One girl had fallen under a table. A boy was letting himself be led out between two friendly shoulders.

'If you don't believe in the resurrection of the dead, come here at closing time,' read a plaque up behind the bar.

—Are you here for long?

—Sorry?

—I'm asking if you're here for long.

The Belfast accent – that incomprehensible, impossible accent the first time you hear it, when two is not pronounced as 'two', but 'toïye', when house is a 'highse', when small is 'wee', when yes is pronounced 'aye', and goodbye, 'cheerio'.

—Are yee hir fer long?

Just a few days. I came for Easter.

—Easter, repeated my traitor.

Already, he was somewhere else. A man at a table had shouted his name.

—Tyrone!

My traitor went off just like that, without so much as a word. He crossed the floor with his arm out, ready to embrace the man who had called him.

Jim was waiting for me, sitting on the edge of a table. Cathy was finishing a drink that wasn't hers. I glanced at my shoes, one lace undone and those negligent stains.

—Time now, ladies and gents! shouted the barmen, piling empty glasses along their arms, right up over their heads.

—Were you with Tyrone Meehan?

—Who's that?

I had got used to Jim's accent, and Cathy's. I don't know why. They had a slower delivery. As though they made an effort for me. When Jim talked to me, I understood almost everything. Not everything, but almost. I stared at his lips, trying to translate, even if some words before and after got lost on the way all the same.

—Have you never heard tell of Tyrone Meehan?

At that moment, by Jim's voice, Jim's eyes, his mouth that told of the respect for the name uttered, I knew that my traitor was one of those whom rebel songs celebrate. His name was Tyrone Meehan. Tyrone Meehan, who had explained to me that to piss like a man, you had to accept to show yourself like a man. Standing back from the urinal, looking elsewhere, hand outstretched, a forgotten cigarette in the corner of your mouth.

That night, Cathy, Jim and I walked home. Back up a deserted Falls Road, misty-wet with rain. How I love thinking about that moment when I am in Paris, hunched over a violin, watching the shadows in my street. We went past two British army jeeps and one foot patrol. Four soldiers walked in front, faces blackened, wearing camouflage and helmets, pointing their guns straight out into the night, and two others walked behind, backwards, kneeling down and taking aim at the sound of Irish voices going past. In the streets, behind the fences, dogs barked. From a window, a guy shouted something I didn't understand. A girl was singing out of tune somewhere, far off in another street. The Brits were coming towards us. As they approached, Jim took me by the arm to cross the road. Nothing ostensible. Just the pressure of his fingers on my sleeve.

One evening, he had explained to me that the Irish Republican Army was there, everywhere, keeping watch over its territory. If this patrol were attacked, it wouldn't do for a Jim, a Cathy, or an Antoine from Paris to stagger along between the sniper and his target. The IRA therefore asked its people to change footpath when enemy soldiers were approaching.

It is said that after the death of a child, hit by an armoured jeep in front of his house, the inhabitants of the street repainted their house fronts. All the facades painted white in one evening, from the ground up to the height of a man. The next day, there was a long, bright strip all along the street, two metres high. It was the month of May. Two nights later, a Scottish Para was killed by a single bullet in the throat by a roof sniper. It was then, searching the low houses one by one and roughly interrogating the population, that the soldiers realized: in this street of broken lamp posts, intruders had to stand out from the dark. They couldn't be mistaken for a passer-by, for a neighbour in a hurry; they couldn't be confused with the darkness of the bricks. They had to be visible, all this whiteness had to show them up and offer them to the gun. British soldiers became shadows, therefore targets, therefore dead. The people had repainted the walls of their street so that no enemy would escape from there again.

—Did I never introduce you to Tyrone?

I said no. I watched the soldiers watching us. They were young. They were tense. They were silent. A hidden radio crackled. Jim was staggering. Cathy was putting her shoe back on. The street was quiet; the club far behind us, the windows deserted. The last black taxis drove slowly past. A few shouts here, a drunken clamour there. The wind. A seagull from the docks. The orange hue of the streetlights. The grease-stained fish-and-chip wrappers rolling around on the pavement. The helicopter. It seemed to shadow us, always, everywhere, far off, with its noisy blades and bright beam of light. It wasn't following us; not particularly. But it was always watching us. And perhaps watching me, too, the Frenchman walking with Jim and Cathy, who had just met the great Tyrone Meehan.

We went into the living room. Jim sat in his armchair. The remains of turf and coal were smoking in the grate. Just the remains of those beautiful flames that had turned to grey when we came in from the rain. It was damp and cold in the room.

I have always known that house this way, with the air bubbles in the wallpaper, water running in rivulets down the bathroom walls, the big cracks in the ceiling, and the window pane of my bedroom replaced by cardboard. It was a simple house, a working-class house, made of dirty bricks and a slate roof, stuck to an identical house, and to another, and to another, and to yet another. An infinite row, winding, Catholic, and dreary. On the opposite side of the street they were the same, and the same in the nearby dead end, and in the next street, in all the streets around here. One door opened out onto the street; a second door, a glass one, opened into the living room and the stairs that led up. The living room was narrow. A television on a coffee table, a fabric sofa, an armchair and a dresser. On the wall, there was a photo of Pope Paul VI in a gold frame, a picture of the Sacred Heart and a poster of Paris rooftops that they had brought back from their honeymoon. Behind the living room, a tiny kitchen. Just a sink, a fridge and a gas oven. No table. In Jim and Cathy's house, you put your plate on your knees. A door gave out onto a garden, a tiny wasteland, closed off by a wooden fence topped with barbed wire. The toilet was out there. A shed, a hole in a cement vat and a spade to spread the lime.

Upstairs, there were two bedrooms. Theirs and mine, when I came here. Since the death of their son, Denis, they had changed nothing. I slept in his little bed. His drawings were yellowing on the walls. His photo was everywhere. He had been killed by a plastic bullet in 1974. He was twelve years old. Since then, Jim and Cathy had been living on their own. At first, they didn't want to have any more children. And then they tried. For a long time. And then they gave up. Cathy went for tests; Jim refused. He said they had suffered too much, that his desire for love had been buried with Denis.

I had pulled an old jumper over my own one. I was absently rubbing my hands above the cold hearth. Jim had kept his jacket on. When it was very cold, he would sometimes even wear his coat in the house. He turned on the television. Cathy made tea. I hate tea. I have never understood tea. Each time, everywhere, as soon as I step inside anywhere in this country, a woman holds a cup of tea out to me. So I drank Cathy's tea. I watched her wrap herself up in a large brown tartan blanket. I watched the images flashing on the television and the plastic Virgin Mary that was flashing on and off at our window.

—Tyrone Meehan is a veteran, said Jim, setting down his cup.

—A veteran of what, I asked.

—Of everything. Of all combats, of everything that means that we can drink this tea calmly, and almost safely.

That night, I was tired. It was a pity. I liked it when Jim talked. But I was barely listening. The journey, the beer, the piss, the hatred and glee we felt when coming across a foreign patrol in this city I wanted to call my own. Jim was sitting in his armchair, with Cathy balancing on the arm, and I was hunched up on the floor beside my chair because everything was lurching. And Jim told me about Tyrone.

JAMES CONNOLLY

I first encountered the Irish Republic in Paris, one November morning in 1974. Under the gaze of a smiling man wearing a round-collared shirt. The lad who showed me the photo used to come into my workshop a lot. He would just drop in, without an appointment, without knocking, and sometimes for no reason. He would push open the door, case in hand, pull out a stool and sit beside me.

His name was Pierre though he preferred to be called Pêr. He was Breton. He came from Plouarzel, which he spelt Plouarzhel. He taught English. He hated England because he loved Ireland.

While I worked, Pêr would talk. He talked and talked and talked. He would make grand, lively gestures, much too big for my silence. Sometimes, he would go to the window and look warily out at my street, as if he were afraid of being followed. He was a nice young man, and a bad violinist. In fact, I don't think he was interested in music. He was not attracted to notes, but to identity.

He thought belonging, not harmony. Pêr was in love with the Irish and the violin made him feel close to them. To find a place between them, squashed onto the end of a bench, to mix his music with the music of pubs. In Derry, he was 'the Breton with the violin'.

'If you throw a stone through a pub window, you'll injure two poets and three musicians', says the Irish proverb. And Pêr was looking for those injuries. Because Pêr's Ireland was not mine. Not yet. My Ireland was *The Quiet Man*, *The Purple Taxi*, the Emerald Isle, Aran jumpers, whiskey, the Éire of our crosswords. It was like a glossy picture. It was green grass, red-haired Maureens, stone walls, thatched roofs and Georgian doors. It was happy, laughing, smoky, black with porter and white with sheep wandering round winding roads. My Ireland – I had been there three times – was Dublin, Galway, Clifden, Lisdoonvarna, Aran. An Ireland that was musical, maritime, agricultural, welcoming, spiritual, poor yet proud, tranquil.

—Do you not know the North? Pêr asked me that November morning in 1974.

I replied that I didn't.

—Then you don't know Ireland, smiled the Breton.

And then he opened his case.

I was leaning over a violin. I was sanding down the upper nut. A slow and silent moment, just before I apply my linen oilcloth.

—Can you have a look at this? It sounds raw. I think it has come unstuck.

I took the Breton's instrument. I shook it upside down to release the dust and hair that had accumulated there. I knocked on the belly with my index finger. It made a noise. An appalling echo. As though something was moving on the inside.

—Perhaps, I said.

But no. Nothing. I had made a mistake. Pêr played his instrument proudly. His fingers touched the fingerboard so hard he almost bruised the ebony. Pulled from its mortise, the hair fluttered on the bow. He did not play, he fought. The wood of his violin bore the hallmarks of battle. Scrapes on the belly, injuries on the ribs, snicks on the pegs, dented nose, the back grated with anger. And a loose chin rest.

—It's the chin rest, I said.

That was all. Nothing more. Loosened by the strength of time, it was wandering over the wood, adulterating the sound.

I tightened the chin rest and got up. With one hand I swept away the sawdust that had fallen onto my knees. I tapped my tuning fork off the side of the workbench. And then I stroked the four strings one after the other. Nothing else was wrong. There was that beautiful tune. I asked Pêr to play. He pulled a sceptical face. He rubbed his hands, pressed his instrument against a green cloth and looked at the ground. Then he breathed in. He banged out a few violent notes. A *gavotte* from the Bas-Léon. His feet tapping on the ground, his mouth in a grimace and his eyes closed. It was a war tune. Another world, suddenly. The Breton armies pitted against the Montparnasse battlements.

—It's still not right, he said, handing it back to me.

I asked him to leave it with me until that evening. I would loosen it a little and remove a small shaving from the sound post. Nothing, just a grain of spruce peeled off with a penknife to show that something had been done.

Pêr was tired. I had repeatedly told him that tiredness spoils the sound of an instrument. That the ear does not capture the same impressions after a sleepless night, five beers or a long day of silence. Pêr said that might be the case, but still. He said I would have to take a better look.

—Can I leave my case?

—On the table over there.

He opened it and put his cloth in it. On the inside, the Breton had made his own lining from threadbare velvet in the colours of the Irish flag. The green, white and orange that made such an impression in the pubs. When he played, he left his case open alongside him. Inside the lid, he had stuck a black-and-white photo of a man in a shirt and waistcoat with a slightly receding hairline, thick eyebrows and a heavy moustache. It looked as though the man was smiling. He was wearing a round-collared shirt.

—Let me introduce you to James Connolly, said Pêr, lifting the case up to eye level.

—A violinist? I asked.

Pêr laughed.

—He could have been but he wasn't. He was an Irish patriot. He was shot in 1916 by the British after the Easter Rising. He had taken over the General Post Office in Dublin with his men and made it the headquarters. And it all went arwy.

I just caught a glimpse of his face before the Breton closed the lid of his case and left the room.

So I began to sand down the nut, slowly, leisurely, in the new-found silence, before taking up the Breton's violin. I inserted a retriever through the f-holes, and removed the small sound post by wetting it against the tip of my lips. Spruce needs to be damp to work on. A flick of the penknife, nothing more, would do it. It was just a shaving, a fragment of nothing. Then I rubbed a little chalk onto the injury before putting the cylinder of wood back into place, to the left of the bass bar, scarcely higher than it had been.

And then, I don't know why, I left my workstation, went over to Pêr's violin case and lifted the lid.

I had already forgotten the name of that man in the round-collared shirt. I rarely remember names. I do remember faces, handshakes, the feel of a person's skin, stories, attitudes, happiness, cruelty, days and nights, but not names. I looked more closely at him: the heavy dark woollen coat, the two waistcoat buttons that caught a flash of light, the tie and the old shirt. He could have been a scholar, or a politician, or even a schoolmaster. Maybe he was not actually smiling. But still. There were those prominent cheekbones and chin, that amused look that wandered from his eyes across his face.

Shot dead.

This man had been shot dead by the English. They had shot dead this politician, this schoolmaster. They had shot dead this stranger in the round-collared shirt. And my life was about to take a new turn.

It was absurd.

If Pêr had tightened his chin rest. If he hadn't come in through the door of the workshop that day. If he hadn't opened his violin case. If he hadn't introduced me to an Irishman who had died fifty-eight years earlier, I would never have gone to Belfast. I would never have walked alongside Jim and Cathy in the threatening night. I would never have met my traitor.

∼

The man in the round-collared shirt was called James Connolly. Again, I found out his name, learned it and committed it to memory. Today, I can even write it in Irish: Séamas Ó Conghaile. Less than five months after the Plouarzel gavotte played by Pêr in my workshop, I hung a photo of the Irish trade unionist up on my wall. The same one that was inside the Breton's violin case, one of those rare photos of Connolly, in a gilded frame, above my workbench among the peg-hole reamers, the files and the bridges, hung by a wire like a maple necklace.

It was May 1975. To celebrate my thirtieth birthday, I travelled to Dublin to meet Yvon, a childhood friend who had married Siobhan, an Irish girl. He was born in Gérardmer. I was born in Besançon. At seventeen, we were both apprentices at the same workshop in Mirecourt in the Vosges mountains. Places had become scarce. Erstwhile capital of violin-making, the town had seen its factories close down one after the other. After the war, in those forests wounded by bombs, the trees on the slopes were no longer worth anything. The pines were mutilated, ploughed, bleeding everywhere. Master violin-makers left the slow ways of the violin, the viola or the mandolin, to make wooden boxes for radios. For three years, Yvon and I worked side by side. I did not speak much. He did not speak at all. My idols were Jean-Baptiste Vuillaume and Etienne Vatelot, legendary violin-makers. His idols were Dominique Peccatte or Jacques Lafleur, renowned bow-makers. I became a violin-maker. He became a bow-maker. It was thanks to Yvon the bow-maker that I came to Ireland. All he has ever really known of this country, even now, are his wife, the beer and the music.

My thirtieth birthday party was fantastic. I actually played my violin – I, who dislike playing in public. Drunk, I played 'O'Keefe's Slide', dreaming of the great Michael Coleman. The next day, very early, I wandered the streets of Dublin. It was a Sunday. I was alone with my bag, my violin case, a queasy stomach and a pounding head. I was to take the plane back in the afternoon, but before that I wanted to roam around Connolly Station. Why those streets? I do not know. I liked their poverty, that cold grey silence. I liked the faces passed. Harsh faces. Lost in their thoughts. Their dark or red hair. Their worn-out clothes, oversized coats and their soft shoes. It was raining. I think I have always seen Dublin through rain. I went into Connolly Station. Just like that, just to have a look. The ticket desks were deserted. A train was waiting at Platform 2. It was going to Drogheda, Newry and Belfast. Just names on a board. I don't know what or why. I went up to the ticket desk. A smiling young woman made me repeat my question three times. I bought a return ticket to Belfast.

—You don't know the North? Then you don't know Ireland, Pêr had said.

And that stupid remark had annoyed me. Heading towards Belfast, I kept my head pressed against the ice-cold window. The carriage was practically empty. The villages and towns were deserted. When the train stopped at the border, two men got on. A controller and a policeman. They passed through without a word, without a glance at the bags or the lowered eyes. And then the train moved off again. I saw a British flag flying from the top of a warehouse. A torn flag, ravaged by time and weather. This is it, I thought. Here I am. I'm in Northern Ireland. I looked at the narrow houses, the trees, the sky, the barbed wire, the iron gates, bottle shards on the tops of walls. I looked at the chimneys; the grey smoke aligned rooftop after rooftop.

I only stayed in Belfast for three hours. Just long enough to walk into the city centre, then to Castle Street, then to the Falls Road. Here, too, everything was like a Sunday. The air was thick with turf and coal. The smell of Belfast. In winter, in autumn, and even when the rain is icy cold, I close my eyes and I succumb to the smell of this city. A mixture of burning hearths, children's milk, earth, fried food and damp.

Near the tall Divis Tower, I saw my first British patrol. I saw my first gun. The soldier was young, crouched down in a garden, behind the gate of a house. I remember his face, a gloomy expression somewhere between fear and boredom. He looked at my violin case. I felt something tremendous and ridiculous. I was happy to be there. Proud to know I was where it was all happening. Dublin seemed far away to me. Another country, almost. Two helicopters dirtied the low sky. Armoured vehicles were constantly driving past. I was on the Lower Falls Road. The streets still bore the wounds of 1969. To terrorize the Catholic population, the Protestant crowd had assembled to the east, in the middle of the night, before charging at the area with burning torches. The inhabitants had been driven away, their homes burnt out. People were killed. Six years later, those wounds were still gaping. Long blackened streets, roofless houses bricked up with breeze-blocks. A desert of charred bricks, bent girders, black wood and refuse. At the corner of a street, I saw two children emerge, throw a stone at the grey hull of an armoured vehicle and run away.

—Are you looking for something? a woman asked me.

She was carrying a shopping bag, wearing a scarf on her head. She thought I was lost. I told her that I was French. The two kids came out from the shadows. So did a tall man whose trousers were too short.

—A Frenchman, said the woman.

The children asked me if I was a journalist. I replied that I was not. They wanted me to open my violin case. The tall man advised me to do it. The woman drew nearer. We were in the middle of the street, at the foot of a big burnt wall, in the wind. It started to rain. I opened my case. A few drops splattered on the varnished wood. In the distance, a siren wailed. I put my violin away. The tall man asked if I would like a cup of tea. I looked at him. A white scar was etched on his forehead. He had a broken nose. I said yes. His house was nearby.

—Cathy, I found a Frenchman, said Jim O'Leary.

It was she who opened the door to us. She smiled. I was welcome. Just like that. Welcome for nothing, just welcome. I sat down in Jim's armchair. With my few words of English, I explained about having been in Dublin, my birthday, what I did for a living. Cathy and Jim listened attentively. They asked me what I thought of the situation. I did not know what to answer. Jim said I had plenty of time to come to understand. It was all simple, intimate, warm. Jim showed me a wooden harp on the mantelpiece. A sculpture with the words 'Long Kesh 1973' engraved on the base. He told me he had been in prison. That this harp was a souvenir of his captivity, something he had made in a workshop.

Above the mantelpiece, there was the photograph of a child, enlarged, in a dark wooden frame. It was Cathy who told me about Denis. Jim leaned against the wall, watching his wife tell me about their son. Denis had been killed in October 1974, just out there, on the corner of their street. A riot had been brewing. Crowds of young nationalists were attacking British armoured cars all over the place. Bricks; bottles on fire. It was dark.

Denis went to buy a pint of milk on the other side of the avenue. A dozen children were running after an armoured car, throwing stones at it. Denis ran across the road in the thick of the unrest. The armoured car stopped abruptly. A soldier came out of the back. He knelt down, placed his rifle on his shoulder and aimed at the children. He fired two plastic bullets. Creamy-grey cylindrical projectiles, twelve centimetres long, three centimetres in diameter, heavy, compact and hard. Jim heard the shots, too close for comfort. He came running out of the house. He got to the end of the street just as the children were scattering. Denis was lying on his front on the footpath. A bullet had hit him above the eye. His face was all smashed up. The armoured car had gone. Other children were bombarding it from another street. When the ambulance came, Denis was still holding the milk money tight in his hand. The doctors could do nothing. Cathy and Jim O'Leary's son died at the Royal Victoria Hospital on 10 October 1974, after six days of agony.

The child's face smiled for a long time on the wall opposite their house. There were other murals on the bricks of that neighbourhood. War paintings. Clandestine soldiers with their guns held high. The faces of the heroes of the Republic: Pearse, Plunkett, my big man in the round-collared shirt. And then there was Denis O'Leary, his little face greeting his parents every morning on the threshold of the street. The mural was repainted once, then twice, and then time went by. One morning, when Jim came out, some young Republicans were stirring the paint in their buckets. It was they who preserved the memory of the walls. Denis's smile was faded. His blond hair greyed by the rain. As they did in all nationalist ghettoes, the police would pass through like a whirlwind, throwing bags of coloured paint onto the fragile artwork. Two blue explosions were soiling Denis's forehead and another, a yellow one, was spreading out like a stain over his eye. Jim went over to the young lads. He looked at his spattered son, then at the sky, then the street. He put his fists in his pockets. He said that it ought to be left like that. That it was enough. That the wall would end up reclaiming its bricks. That his son's face should be left to slowly fade.

Jim listened to Cathy telling me about Denis. His face was different. Her face was too. There was grief in her eyes, on her brow, even in her voice. An infinite hardness. I would learn to know these faces, year after year, in anger and in tragedy. I would see them everywhere. I would recognize them. Each Irish person I would meet would one day wear this war mask. Cathy kissed the tips of her fingers and gently touched the photo of their son. And then she smiled at me. Everything in her had become silent again.

We exchanged addresses. Cathy and Jim had come to Paris for their honeymoon. They knew Montmartre, the Moulin-Rouge and the *Mona Lisa*. Jim shook my hand on the doorstep. As I was turning the corner of his street, he stopped a friend's car with a short whistle. He leaned through the window and said a few words to the driver.

—This is Brian. He'll take you back.

Brien was quiet all the way to the station. I sat beside him. I looked at his tattoos. The tricolour of the Republic, the blue letters 'IRA' and the picture of a harp covered with brambles were tattooed onto his forearms. We overtook British armoured trucks, went past patrols. Jim had advised me not to speak French if we were stopped. To act like them in front of the soldiers. Like all Irish people. A sullen face and eyes looking elsewhere, hands in pockets, head down, lips pursed.

Arriving at the station, I noticed a handful of tracts pushed into the door pocket. One of them had almost fallen out of the car. It was hanging out of the door. I took it.

—Keep it, Brian told me.

It was information about a memorial service. Just the time of the meeting, the place and a photo of James Connolly. The Irishman with the round-collared shirt. I found this extraordinary. The man had left Pêr's violin case. He was everywhere, all around Ireland. And in my pocket too. On the platform at the station, I opened my violin case and slipped the tract in flat, so as not to damage it.

The trip home was interminable. And the return to Paris, even a little bit painful. I did not go back home. I went straight to my workshop. I don't know why. I didn't want to wait until Monday morning. I wanted James Connolly to take his place. Not yet in a frame, but already on my wall. With his heavy coat, his waistcoat, his moustache, his calm expression, a little bit of the hills of Belfast, Brian's silence, Jim's smiles, Cathy's tea, the clamour of the boy's stone against the British armoured truck, the accent of the woman in the street, the rain, the throbbing of the helicopters, the poverty of the bricks, and the gun.

I carefully cut the tract and kept only the photo, surrounded by black. I stuck it on the wall with two drops of varnish. I switched everything off and I sat down. My workshop is a small room on the ground floor of a building, with a window looking out onto the street. It was night. Everything was dark. There was only the red and green neon light of the hotel opposite, caressing James Connolly's face.

A TERRIBLE BEAUTY

I saw Tyrone Meehan again on Easter Sunday 1977, the day after we first met. I didn't recognize him. He was in the middle of the street, his back to me, his hands in his pockets, the hood of his blue parka coming down over his eyes. He was speaking to two men in a low voice. When I drew near, he called me over.

—Son?

With a flick of his thumb, the Irishman pulled back his hood. He winked at me, smiling, with that slight movement of the head that people do here to say hello. With a nod, he introduced me to Tim Devlin and Mike O'Doyle. He told them that I was French, and a violin-maker. People were greeting us from all around. It was early afternoon. It was raining. Hundreds of nationalists were arriving on the Falls Road. Men in their cheap Sunday best, women done up to the nines. Young girls wore the colours of the Republic in their hair. It was the first time I had celebrated the Easter Rising of 1916. The previous year, I had gone back before the procession.

Tyrone Meehan watched the parade fall into place. Mike O'Doyle said nothing. He was a big man, slightly hunched, with a hard face and very bright eyes. He was on his guard, looking around all the time. The other one, Tim Devlin, spoke fast. I didn't understand everything he said. Several times, the word 'Ra' had stood out from a whisper. 'Ra', for 'Republican Army'. I would soon start calling the IRA that, like everyone else. At one point, Tyrone moved off towards a group of men standing against a pub wall.

—Are you coming, wee Frenchman?

I turned up the collar of my jacket and followed him. He approached the group. He leaned in towards one of the men, who spoke quietly, pointing to a street across the way. Then Tyrone nodded. He winked at me and asked me to go to the corner of that street and wait.

—Wait for what? I asked.

—It's a surprise, replied the Irishman, putting his hand on my shoulder.

At the corner of the street, I saw Mike. He was chatting to an old lady who was holding onto his arm. Republicans were arriving from everywhere. Whole families; dozens of prams. I looked at each face, each smile, each flag, each lapel sporting a paper lily, the symbol of the rebels. I had pinned mine on the previous night to go to the club. My Easter lily was crumpled and faded; it still bore the pinhole from last year, but I didn't want another one. An old man had given it to me. He had taken it from his coat and pinned it on mine. Because I was French and because I was leaving before the parade. Wearing this green, white and gold symbol had been my first gesture of belonging.

The rain had stopped. In the middle of the street, assembled on pavements, perched up on poles, railings and roofs, thousands of Irish people were waiting. When the British armoured jeeps appeared, the crowd jeered them. That was all. No stones are thrown on this day. Quite simply, James Connolly and his round-collared comrades are honoured. From a Land Rover, a policeman with a loudspeaker was saying that the gathering was illegal. A sign on the side of the jeep read 'Please disperse'. Men spat on the ground. Children gave them the finger. Beside me, a woman cried out to the police to go back to where they came from.

—This is my home here! shouted one man.

It was routine. The Brits reminded them that the parade was banned, but did nothing to really stop it. There were too many children, too many elders, too many people to plough through the crowd. The armoured jeeps left in a blaring cloud of diesel fumes.

When the huge clamour broke out, I had my back to the road. The crowd was cheering at something behind me that I could not see. Flags were being vigorously waved, men were standing with their clenched fists raised, hundreds of children were shouting with joy.

—IRA! IRA!

The first volunteer of the Irish Republic was a few yards away from me. My first one. He was wearing a black beret, black glasses, a black tie, a black jacket with a large black belt, black trousers and white gloves. He was leading his troops in the marching. Twenty or so women and men walking up the narrow street in three rows, one after the other.

—Left! Left! Left, right, left! the officer was shouting.

My fists were clenched. My vision was blurred. My mind was numb. I watched the joy, the laughter, the waving hands, the war march. I let myself get caught up in it. Without these well-pressed black uniforms, the crowd would have looked as though it were welcoming a carnival parade, or a cycling race, or celebrating a popular singer. Nothing spoke of the pain. All the sadness, the distress, all that stank of fear and death, was wiped out by the volunteers' footsteps.

Behind this little troop, the locals were joining the parade. In three rows, like their soldiers, with no banners or slogans. Silence had returned. The crowd was stern, compact, beautiful and proud. They seemed so fragile against the British armoured jeeps, with their clenched fists, their insults and their angry eyes. But when the volunteers took the lead, the people held their heads high. Beside me, an old man had put his walking stick under his arm, like an officer's cane. Another kept shouting 'Our boys are here,' winking all around him. On the footpaths, children were no longer talking. I watched them standing there, with that intense look in their eyes and their mouths gaping before such a treat. Cathy and Jim had not arrived yet. They were doing what hundreds of others were doing, waiting for the parade to pass the end of their street and then joining in. Even now, many Sundays after that Sunday, I still tremble when I watch this ceremonial, repeated each year to celebrate the taking of the General Post Office in Dublin. The dogged crowd that walks up the Falls Road, nourished by silence, street after street, year after year.

—Are you all right, son?

Tyrone did not stop. He turned towards the soldiers. Standing to attention, his hand in the air, he ordered them to straighten up the rows. Other men in the crowd, tense, caps tightly fitted, hoods up, seemed to be on guard in small groups.

—The IRA is also made up of those who remain unseen, Jim had explained.

I walked up along the parade, which had come to a halt. Standing in front of the commander and his troops, seven volunteers bore the colours of the Republic. Seven big flags, flapping in the wind and the rain. I knew the first one, the green, white and gold national emblem. I also knew those of the four Irish provinces: the red hand of Ulster, the three crowns of Munster, the golden harp of Leinster and the eagle and sword of Connaught. It was Jim who explained the other banners to me, the starry plough flag that honours Connolly's socialism, and the rising sun of Na Fianna Éireann, the Republican youth.

Behind the IRA, ex-prisoners had got into line. Hundreds of them, three to a row. Women, men, some barely adults, some grey- and white-haired. I knew a few of them. They would get together at the club to talk quietly, and then more volubly as the beer took hold. The families of prisoners and victims came next. Women without husbands, children without fathers, men with nothing left at all. I stood for a long time looking at this colourless mass. They all had the same look on their faces. I couldn't meet their gaze. There was something in their eyes like the early morning mist that lingers, something sad and weary. The women had wrapped their hair in scarves, away from the rain. Their clothes were threadbare, their hands red with cold. I walked amongst them, brushing gently past.

A young girl looked at me for a long time. Like others, she wore a crown of flowers. She made a sign, with a look in her eyes that told me it was going to be all right. That I shouldn't be worried. That this was just the way things were: war, poverty, prison, death. And that I just had to keep faith. And that I mustn't cry, since nobody here was crying.

I *was* crying.

I hadn't felt it coming. Neither the stinging feeling before the tears, nor their path down my cheeks, nor their sad taste. I watched these dreary shadows, these muddy clothes, these messy heads of hair, these orphan mouths, these tired backs, these eyes deprived of horizons.

The crowd moved forward, traipsing slowly, sinuously, between the low houses, the bricks, the smashed-up footpaths, the walls and more walls again. I climbed up onto a cement block. People were marching as far as the eye could see. An army of misery. I followed the march from the footpath. I had decided to slip in beside Jim and Cathy when it reached them. Two helicopters surveyed our progression. Nobody talked. They were just marching, to the sound of the warrior drums and fifes.

I caught sight of Tyrone again when we reached Milltown Cemetery. He was grouping together over a hundred women in front of the monument to the Republican dead. Cathy had joined them. Jim was walking beside me between the leaning tombstones and the weeds. I had never seen such a cemetery. At nightfall when the sky over Ireland gives itself over to greys and blacks, in the wind, in the rain, when a thin ray of light slices the sooty clouds, it looks like a wasteland. A chaos of celtic crosses, brambles and muck sloping down towards the edge of the city. I stood with my back against a granite angel. Into the microphone, a man spoke about Dublin, of the taking of the GPO by the insurgents, of the defeated rebellion, of the injured James Connolly, shot dead sitting on a chair on 12 May 1916. And of the others, the Republican leaders, dragged one by one to the post in the courtyard of Kilmainham Gaol.

—Thomas Clarke, Sean MacDiarmada, Thomas MacDonagh, Padraig Pearse, Eamonn Ceannt, Joseph Plunkett, the man intoned.

Then, five IRA volunteers raised their joined hands up towards the sky. Around me, women put their hands over their ears. Children were hoisted up onto their fathers' shoulders. Older men and women pulled back. I had never seen weapons in action before. A hunting rifle, maybe, but never a real weapon. The officer gave an order. The soldiers fired. Once, twice, three times. I could see the steel against their white gloves. After each salute, two young boys picked up the fire-hot shells and gave them to Mike O'Doyle. I had never heard the noise of war, that scream of scathing metal. I gave a violent start. I bit the inside of my cheek. After the national anthem, Tyrone stood in front of the group of women he had assembled. At his signal, they suddenly put up their umbrellas. All at the same time. A hundred umbrellas held out, some raised towards the sky like a roof, others held out like a screen. Cathy was facing us, hidden by her red umbrella. The IRA volunteers broke rank. They ran in amongst the women, behind the umbrellas. Mothers and their prams followed suit. The helicopters still circled, lower than the clouds.

—What's going on? I asked Jim.

—It's a magic trick, smiled the Irishman.

The umbrellas closed. The Republican Army had disappeared. All that remained among the buggies and the laughing women were local men. No weapons, not a single uniform. Just a wife on her husband's arm, a father pushing a pram, three friends messing around, a grumpy old man putting his cap back on, a couple in each other's arms, just as if they were coming out of a pub. And the crowd, all around them, began to walk back towards the cemetery gates; it drew closer, gave way, and took them back into its midst, one by one.

∼

Jim parted the curtains with one finger, ever so slightly, so he could see without being seen.

—Switch off the light, he said in a low voice.

I liked that worried grey look, that tension that creased his forehead. He was at the corner of the window, flattened against the wall. He watched the street. A British patrol had stopped there, just outside the front door. From the living room, I could hear the crackling of their army radio. He gestured at me to move closer. The street lamps gave the night an orange hue. A soldier was kneeling against the wall. He was pointing his gun towards the rooftops, his eye against the viewscope. Another one was lying on the footpath. People were passing by without so much as a glance. Others crossed over. After a few minutes, an armoured jeep arrived. The Brits got in through the rear, running backwards.

—Bastards! Jim said.

He said it suddenly, like when he spat on the ground or slammed his fist on a table. He switched the light back on. Cathy had made sandwiches and tea.

—Are they gone?

—They're gone, her husband replied.

As soon as the jeep rounded the corner, the guests arrived. It was as though they had been waiting for the patrol to leave before knocking on the door. There was a couple I had seen at the club, a young man who had been at the cemetery, two prisoners' wives and, finally, Tyrone Meehan and Sheila, his wife.

—They're all over the place tonight, Tyrone said, taking off his coat.

—Everywhere, Jim smiled.

I had bought four bottles of Guinness and a bottle of orangeade. That's the way things are done here. Each person brings their own drink. The orangeade was extra. Out of a brown paper bag, Tyrone took out some Harp, a light beer that is very easy to drink. Sheila had a naggin of white rum in her pocket. The young man had bought a bottle of wine in my honour. A bottle of Piat d'Or, presented on the label as 'The most famous wine in France'. I had had a head start: three bottles of stout since the beginning of the evening. I was sitting in my usual place, on the floor, my back against the

the armchair. The television was on. The news showed only a few shots of the Easter march – the IRA, not the crowd – and these were accompanied by an English commentary on sectarianism and violence. Jim switched it off.

Tyrone had a glass of beer in his hand. He raised it to eye level and winked at me. It was almost warm. I felt at home among the smell of tea and toast, in the laughter that followed one of Jim's stories. Everyone had their own anecdote. They all spoke so fast I had trouble following. One of the guests, a redhead, was saying that yesterday morning, in the little corner shop, there were only prisoners' wives, like herself. Five Republican women, with the same list of authorized products for the men's visitors' room in their hands. Tea, three oranges, two apples, a few bits of chocolate. And the cashier putting through the same articles each time, without a word. When her turn came, the redhead had a big bag of sweets in her basket.

—Is that allowed? asked the cashier.

—No, that's for me, replied the woman.

Cathy laughed. Tyrone raised his glass. He asked after Paddy Nooley, who had just been released the day before from Long Kesh. Jim said that he was doing all right. I was getting frustrated. I only understood one in four words. At one point, Jim mimed something for me: he got up, kneeled down and placed an imaginary rocket launcher on his shoulder. Everyone laughed again. Cathy translated in slower English. Paddy Nooley had just done nine years for having launched a bazooka back to front. That was at the end of the 1960s.

There had been a shortage of weapons. To reassure the population on Saturday nights in the streets of Belfast, the volunteers would pass three or four old standard-issue English pistols from one to the other. Tyrone Meehan told me about it. One night he had knelt on the Falls Road, at the corner of Cavendish Street, a Webley in his hand, finger on the trigger, in the position of a gunman at ease. He was waiting for a group to go past, revellers young and old, who lowered their voices when they saw him. He was on the watch, at his corner. An old woman whispered to him to hang on in there. A boy murmured 'Up the IRA', raising his fist. Men winked. A woman blessed herself. Another said thank you. Tyrone waited for the group to pass, put his gun inside his jacket and left his post, running, taking the back streets, and gave the weapon to a comrade who was waiting a few dozen metres farther on. When they got to the top of the next street, a volunteer was standing there, masked with a scarf, the Webley pointing towards the ground. And again, further up, elsewhere, even right into the park, the same weapon was passed from glove to glove so that that night, just before they went to bed, a handful of neighbours thought that arms were arriving in Ireland by the shipful.

Paddy Nooley was a plumber and quite the handyman. He had put together a bazooka with a steel tube. He had noticed that the calibre of his weapon was the exact same size as a packet of biscuits he loved. Round butter and lemon biscuits with jagged edges. He needed a wad to hold the charge of his weapon, so he pushed four packets into the rocket launcher. The biscuits were on one side and the projectile on the other. And then it all happened very quickly. Paddy Nooley was young and this was his second operation. A British post guarded the entrance to the nationalist ghetto of Ardoyne. The IRA unit arrived at night. There were four of them. It was Paddy who opened fire. The Irish soldier knelt down on the pavement and fired at the enemy.

Jim was miming the scene. Cathy was wiping her tears as she quietly translated for me. She was laughing. Tyrone was laughing. Sheila was laughing. I was laughing too, just to fit in.

—After the explosion, the Brits came out into the courtyard.

There were biscuit crumbs all over the inside of the station. On the roof, the wire screens, the barbed wire, the sentry box. The whole street smelt of powder and curdled milk. Paddy Nooley stood up. He was shaking. When he had opened fire, he had messed up and fired the weapon the wrong way round. The rocket had hit a wall behind him and he had bombarded the English with biscuits. He was so surprised that he didn't move. He stayed like that, the tube at his feet, looking at the disembowelled wall and the people shouting out their windows, until the soldiers arrested him.

—Having said that, Snoopy didn't do much better, said Tyrone, getting a beer for himself.

Snoopy was on a motorbike behind Jack, who was driving. Snoopy had just shot dead a policeman in Castle Street. Jack was heading back up the Falls Road, zigzagging between the cars. Just as they were taking the turn-off for the Whiterock Road, beside a British roadblock, Snoopy indicated with his right hand. Still holding the gun.

—Jack is Sheila and Tyrone's son, Cathy told me. He got twenty years.

—That's life, Tyrone said abruptly, so they could move on and talk about something else.

And then he sang. Just like that, with no warning. He closed his eyes and sang, sitting on the edge of the sofa.

> You may travel far far from your own native home
> Far away o'er the mountains, far away o'er the foam
> But of all the fine places that I've ever been
> There's none to compare with the Cliffs of Dooneen.

Cathy was the next to sing. A song in Irish I didn't understand. Then Jim sang. So did one of the prisoner's wives. I stood up and opened my violin case. I waited, my instrument on my knees. I felt really at home for the first time. There was no danger, no tension, no holding back, no low voices, no shifty eyes, nothing but these people and their trust in me.

—Your turn, son, Tyrone said.

Cathy was watching me. Jim was drinking slowly. The young man finished off his wine. Sheila passed around cigarettes, three by three in a fan between her fingers. I was trembling. I had already played here and there, for Jim or in a pub, but not like this. Not with this silence facing me. Not with Tyrone Meehan who had cupped his chin in the palm of his hand. Not after these stories, these songs, this shared laughter. I was the French violin-maker. I hardly dared. I put the bow against the strings. I closed my eyes. I wanted to play my best ever. My mouth was dry. I played 'O'Keefe's Slide', a traditional piece. I just let my fingers play away. A few notes out of tune. But it mattered little to me. And I think it mattered little to them. They cheered loudly. Tyrone Meehan put his thumbs up. Later in the kitchen, he told me that Jack's bedroom was free and that I shouldn't think twice about staying there. If Jim and Cathy couldn't put me up for some reason, the bed belonging to his imprisoned child was there for me.

—I'm fond of you, son, said Tyrone, putting his hand on my shoulder.

—I'm fond of you too, I replied, smiling.

—Is that right? And why is that? he asked.

And then he gave his big laugh. It was the first time I had heard it. A marvellous stream of laughter, no holding back. A laugh that I would try to imitate without ever managing to. A laugh that still wakes me up at night now that he is dead.

Back in Paris, I felt it. Waking up day after day, walking in the street that April of 1977, looking up at the sky for no reason, passing by people I didn't know. I was different. I was something more. I had another world, another life, other hopes. I had the taste of bricks, a taste of war, a taste of sadness and of anger too. I cast aside useless music and devoted myself to the melodies of my new country. I began to read. Everything about Ireland. Only about Ireland. Ireland, Ireland, Ireland. I looked for this word in the columns of newspapers, in the ink of books; I read it on people's lips, in people's eyes, everywhere. I learnt that in Irish, for Irish Republican Army you said 'Óglaigh na hÉireann'. I celebrated St Patrick's Day. I coloured my hair green. I read about the Book of Kells, the Viking raids, the battles of Toirdelbach Ua Briain, the king of Munster. I learnt about the Norman invasion, the Gaelic uprising, the Tudor Conquest, the Ulster Plantation, the rebellions that were crushed one after the other, Cromwell's savagery, the defeat of the Catholic James II. I found out about the Penal Laws, the Great Famine, Home Rule. I read in English about the War of Independence, the Civil War, the war in the North. I read O'Brien, O'Flaherty, Beckett, Kavanagh, O'Casey, Behan, Wilde, Synge, Swift. I tried to read Joyce. I cut out part of a poem by Yeats. I stuck it up beside James Connolly on my workshop wall.

> Now and in time to be,
> Wherever green is worn,
> Are changed, changed utterly:
> A terrible beauty is born.

I decided that Guinness would be my *eau de vie*. I found it hard, to begin with. That bitterness, that heavy, earthy, burnt flavour. The unctuousness of its creamy head, the interminable pint. With Jim and Cathy, sitting at a table in the Thomas Ashe, I pretended to enjoy it. I drank without pleasure. But from now on I would find the black beer to my taste. It was a ritual. On the Falls Road, I had bought myself an Aran pom-pom hat. And also a Claddagh ring, the friendship ring that is over 400 years old. A crowned heart held between two hands. The tip pointed inwards towards one's heart whispers that you are taken. The tip pointed outwards avows that you are free. Jim wore a Claddagh; so did Cathy. Tyrone had an old silver one. I looked at people's fingers in pubs, in the streets. I let my hand linger on tables so that my heart could be seen. In the 1970s, Loyalist paramilitaries cut off fingers of those who wore this ring because it said they were Catholic Irish. That was their game. Like engraving the word 'papist' with a knife on the back of a kid swiped at random from the street. One night, in the Parisian metro, I noticed a woman reading. A Claddagh glinted at her ring finger. My mouth was dry and my knees were weak. I put my hand on the pole opposite her, tapping the steel with the gold of my ring, but she did not raise her head.

I decided that I would go to Belfast twice a year. Once for Easter, and again in August, for the commemorative march on the anniversary of the 1971 Internment Without Trial. When Cathy and Jim were not there, I now slept at Tyrone's. I was a little less at ease with him and Sheila, but I found my place. I would bring in coal from the back yard. I filled the stove in the cold early morning. I slept upstairs, in their son's bed. It was also I who locked the forged-iron gate on the stairs that separated the ground floor from the first. One night, I forgot. I had gone to bed late and had had a few drinks. I couldn't find the key. It was the only time I ever saw Tyrone angry. He explained that five Catholics had died because they forgot to lock their gate. Loyalists had broken down the front door with an axe and had rushed upstairs, firing at the beds.

—With the gate, they are blocked downstairs. So they fire a few shots on the staircase, but you get out alive, Tyrone had said.

More and more often, it was he who came to pick me up at the station or at the airport. And it was also he who brought me back again. When we came up to an army checkpoint, he asked me not to speak. And especially not in French. To give neither my name, nor a response to the two questions asked: 'Where are you coming from?', 'Where are you going to?' So I would act just like him. I said nothing. For as long as possible. Until he encouraged me with a look to admit to being a French violin-maker.

—Bastards!

Like Jim, Tyrone spat this word out all the time. Going past a Scottish patrol, observing a helicopter above his city, when a British flag was flying at the top of a flagpole, when the prime minister appeared on television. He would say 'bastards' and spit. So I began spitting too. Even in Paris, without realizing it. I walked the streets as if I owned them, in long strides, my shoulders hunched, fists in my pockets, collar up, and I would spit.

—When I first saw you I thought you were Irish, a girl from Belfast told me one day.

I looked at myself as I passed by a shop window. My tweed jacket was on the small side, my trousers too short, I had a lofty air about me and looked like I was from here. Irish. I had become like them, without wanting to, without changing anything about my attitude. I found something in me that had always been there. Something in me I had never suspected. For a short while, I thought of coming to live in Belfast, leaving behind the little I had in France and working with wood and varnish here, in one of these small brick houses. Become something more, much more. Join up. Help in the Republican combat.

—No.

—Why not?

—Because you are more useful as you are, Tyrone replied.
—As I am?
—As you are.
—What am I?
—A French violin-maker. A good lad. And a friend.

That day, Tyrone Meehan did something terrible. He took me by the shoulders. He looked me right in the eye and asked me never to forget this. I was not Irish. I would never be Irish. I gave him, Sheila, Jim, Cathy, all of them, something other than the support they gave each other from day to day. An attitude that was not from around here, and they needed that. He looked at me as he told me to remain who I was, and that he would never let anyone take advantage of me. I think he knew, then. He didn't say anything else, but I think he knew. He had a pretty good idea that I would soon help the Republican cause. Very little, at that. Here and there. Tiny things, to bring me closer to them. I think he knew, and wanted to protect me, guard me against my enthusiasm and my naïve anger. It was the autumn of 1979, a few weeks before he was to be arrested again. Tyrone Meehan warned me. Tyrone Meehan protected me from himself.

MISE ÉIRE

It was Monday 8 October 1979. Sheila Meehan called me. Her voice sounded frightened on the phone. She didn't say much. 'They came this morning. They've taken Tyrone.' I had just opened my workshop. A tall guy was waiting for me on the pavement, a violin case in his hand. It was the first time I had seen him. He played in a baroque group. He was working on Handel's Sonata in D Major for Violin and Basso Continuo. He was concerned. He took out his violin and handed it to me. He talked about the adagio. He thought his E was too sharp. He also said his D was too full. He wanted it to be more rounded, more resonant, looser, rid of a rich, grainy sound like sand.

—Sand? I asked.

—Sand, the tall guy responded.

That's when the telephone rang. Sheila's voice. The big guy watching me. His violin on the workbench. My trembling hand.

—They took Jim and some other men from the street, too.

—I'll take a flight to Dublin. I'm coming, I told Sheila.

She did not protest. She just whispered her thanks. Then she hung up. I remained like that for a long while, telephone at my ear, its drilling dial tone. 'They have taken Tyrone.' Sheila's voice was all around the amber-coloured wood, the ebony fret, the elegant binding, the delicate f-holes. I ran my finger mechanically along the layer of resin that was fading on the soundboard. The big guy said nothing. I had a penknife in my hand, as cold as a dead bird. I froze. He lowered his shoulders. Without a word, he gently took back his violin, wrapped the scroll in a chamois cloth and put the instrument back in its case. It was an old imitation Guarneri del Gesù, Paganini's Cannon. I didn't have time to get a better look. The big guy left reluctantly. He said goodbye. Or nothing. I don't know. He left the workshop as though it were a funeral parlour.

When I arrived in Belfast, Jim had just been released. He had been arrested in his home the previous night. Cathy, who had tried to intervene, had been hit with the butt of a rifle in the chest. There was an air of tragedy about the place. There were soldiers everywhere. Helicopters, armoured jeeps, patrols. It was raining. There were no children in the streets. The men kept their heads down. The women were shadows.

—Get yourself a room. It's dangerous to stay with us, Jim said.

Cathy knew a widow who rented a room by the day a little farther down, in Cavendish Street. It was just for a few nights. A tiny room, with a bed, a wardrobe and a crucifix. No chair, nothing. The room smelt of poverty and the freezing cold. The old lady boiled water for her ablutions. A board replaced one of my windows. The toilet was out back in the yard, a hole in the ground and some lime.

—Is it not heated? I asked.

—Welcome to the ghetto, Jim smiled, putting my bag on the

bed. Cathy and Jim had been right. The Brits came back to their house the next day, and again the day after that. They searched everywhere, threw everything on the ground. They were looking for something or someone.

When Sheila Meehan opened the door to me, she looked out at the street and then pulled me in by the arm, closing the door again.

—Quick, it's overrun, was all she said.

Tyrone was being held at Crumlin Road Gaol. Sheila knew neither when nor why he would be up in court. She asked me to be careful. The soldiers were talking about a 'Frenchman'. Someone had heard that. I might have to avoid coming to Belfast for a while. She didn't really know. I didn't know either. She asked me if I wanted a cup of tea. I said I didn't. She asked me where I was going to sleep. She nodded. She said that we could maybe see each other the next day in Milltown Cemetery. She had to put flowers on her father's grave. She was afraid. She didn't want me to stay. She had something to give me. A wide and thick brown envelope that she had hidden under one of the sofa cushions. Tyrone had prepared it for me before his arrest. That was all. She shook her head. Didn't want to know. She handed it to me, asking me not to open it there, to slip it into my jacket. She took my hand, smiling sadly. There were tears in her eyes. She told me to be careful. To take care. And she said it again, lifting the curtain, leaning against the window to watch the street. She signalled to me. She opened the door, putting her hand on my back.

It was still raining. I slipped the envelope into my jacket. I looked for a black taxi, one of those old London cabs bought up by the Republican movement. But no black taxis were driving down the Falls Road. The buses were not running either. Night was falling. All I saw was fear. For the first time in my new life, I would rather not have been there. The wind whipped a damp newspaper page up against my leg. An armoured jeep went past, then a second one. There were shouts, the sound of broken bottles, of stones against scrap metal. I put my head down. There I was, walking quickly, my jacket a little on the small side and my trousers too short.

—Stop right there! shouted a man.

It wasn't a voice from around here. It wasn't the accent of these streets. With my head down, I had bumped into a British army checkpoint. Dozens of men in helmets lying in wait beside houses, on the footpaths, in the small gardens, stopping cars and people. Five Irishmen were facing a wall, their foreheads against the brick, arms up and legs apart. A soldier came towards me. From a short distance, he asked me to raise my hands slowly too. I thought of Jim, who had been tortured for four days in Castlereagh Interrogation Centre. His nose had been broken, and his jaw. He was held in a room artificially lit day and night. He was prevented from sleeping. He was not fed. I thought of Tyrone, who had been beaten by army auxiliaries. Beaten so much that he lost some teeth, his hair was pulled out in clumps and his eyes closed over with bruising. I got scared.

—French, I said.

—Reporter?

—No, tourist.

—A tourist?

The brown envelope fell onto the ground. By my feet. It was quite heavy.

—Do not touch anything. Kneel down. Keep your hands in the air.

I did as I was told. Hands up, on my knees, head down.

The soldier lifted up the envelope with the tip of his boot.

—What's this?

—I'm French. I no speak well English.

Two other soldiers approached, as well as a policeman in a green uniform. He took the envelope. He held it with the tips of his gloved fingers and rushed off into a Saracen that was blocking the road. I was still kneeling. I listened to the metallic orders on the radios. Cars leaving. Harsh voices. Insults being shouted from a window just across the way. I waited.

—Let him go, said the policeman.

He held out the opened envelope to me. I got back up.

—For tourism, you're better off going to Spain, laughed a young soldier.

I smiled too. I was trembling. I wanted to be at home, in my workshop, a penknife in my hand and shavings of maple around me. I imagined sinking my penknife into a soldier's neck. I had never felt such anger. Never in all my life. They had hit Cathy with their rifle butts, they had imprisoned the righteous Tyrone Meehan, they had shot dead my great man in the round-collared shirt, and they had smiled at me. I was angry at myself for showing them a polite face. I should have remained with my fists clenched and an unresponsive look. Or else I should have stood up to them, like a dog, teeth bared, threatening, my head held high, and hated them with my silence. I didn't have the courage of this place yet. I was trembling. I went on my way, walking slowly. Armed men had taken over the street. I wanted a safe pass, showing I had already been stopped, that it was over for today, so that I could feel safe. I gave my name twice more. At gunpoint to a policeman and to two soldiers who inspected the envelope.

It was documentation on Michael Coleman, the great Irish violinist born in a Sligo village on 31 January 1891. I had asked Tyrone for this and had forgotten about it. My friend had included an old forty-five and a Franco-English dictionary of lute-making terms. Thanks to these pages, I would know from then on that spruce is *épicéa*, that alder is *aulne*, that birdseye maple is the English for *érable moucheté*, that a plane is *rabot* and a reamer *alésoir*.

∼

In October 1979 I stayed in Belfast for nine days. I waited in vain for Tyrone Meehan to be tried. Each morning, I accompanied Sheila to the entrance of Crumlin Road Gaol to try and get some news. I stayed on the footpath, across the road, my hands in my pockets like the other men hanging around. In the street, the tension was as palpable as ever. Every day, one or two nationalists were brought in. Night-times shattered with brief bursts of gunfire. Sometimes we ran into Republican volunteers. They no longer wore their parade uniforms; just parka hoods pulled down over their faces. They ran from side streets to gardens, an assault rifle or gun in their hands. They jumped over the low front walls of houses, abruptly entering quiet living rooms and leaving by the back doors, deliberately left open. I could feel the war. I could feel it in the smell of coal and turf, of greasy oil and of cold rain. That Belfast smell, that worried taste. It was the first time I had really felt it.

The day before I left, an IRA unit opened fire on a foot patrol in the middle of the day, a few metres from me. I didn't see where the gunshots came from. A soldier fell down beside a wall. He let his rifle fall. A metallic noise. His helmet hit the footpath. The British did not retaliate. They were shouting, their eyes in the gunsights looking at the roofs. A mother took her child into her arms. Another let out a long scream. I hid in the corner of a doorway. The Englishman was lying on his front. Thick blood flowed along the ground. The crowd was hesitant. A policeman fired into the air to disperse us. I ran like the others. I was in a rage. A rage of violence, sadness and joy. They had got one. We had got one. I turned around to see him again. Armoured jeeps were arriving from everywhere, as well as a Land Rover with a red cross slapped on its side.

—Don't run! Walk normally! a young man shouted at us, his arms spread out.

I came to a halt. Soldiers were blocking the road. All I could see were the dead man's boots and the bottom of his fatigues. That was it; he was dead. I read it the next day in the *Irish News*. Steve Remington was from Bramptom, Yorkshire. He had refused to follow his father, his grandfather and the others down the mine. He had joined the army to leave the misery of the miners' terraced houses. He was twenty-three years old.

'Is there a life before death?' asked graffiti on a Falls Road wall. Before I took the train to Dublin, I touched that wall like the wall of a temple. I touched it for a long time, palm flat, to feel the cold of the stone. Further up the street, a British soldier was climbing up an electricity pole to pull down a Republican flag. I almost wanted him to see me. He who was destroying a symbol, I who was feeding off one. The place was throbbing. Tyrone was in prison. In Long Kesh, in that immense prisoner camp built in the middle of the countryside, south of Belfast, 300 Irish Republicans had been naked for three years. Utterly naked. Wrapped in their bed blankets, they refused to wear the same uniform as common-law prisoners. I looked at the photos until they made my head spin. Two of them in particular, caught in their cell by a television camera, thin, their faces covered with hair, giving the rough blankets the elegance of a gown.

I carried this image with me everywhere. In my wallet, in my workshop. My eyes would go from the pale wood to the paler faces. One morning in 1979, to break their resistance, the prison guards refused to let the prisoners slop out. And so they began the dirty protest. They pissed on the ground. They smeared their excrement on the walls of their cells by hand. They shouted that they were political prisoners. Naked and in their shit, their feet covered in urine, no visits, no exercise, no letters, no nothing, alone, for months on end, months that were to stretch into two years.

From above, the buildings of the camp were 'H'-shaped. The white letter soon became the symbol of the Republican martyr. Painted on walls, worn on the back of shirts, stuck up in teenagers' rooms, engraved in stone, branded on wood, shouted by children, repeated infinitely. 'God made us Catholic, guns made us equal', said another wall. Every bullet fired by the free men was a response to the humiliation of the imprisoned.

'And you? What are you doing for the prisoners?' asked a poster in a bar. What was I doing? Absolutely nothing. I was just passing through, walking around in my tweed jacket. I looked if I was being looked at. I put on airs. I looked at photos. I made myself sick with sadness.

Jim drove me to the station. He didn't want me to take a taxi. In the space of a few weeks, two Catholics had been killed by Loyalists in east Belfast, having trusted an unknown driver. We drove slowly. Jim was inscrutable. He kept looking in his rear-view mirror.

—I'll leave you in front of the station, I'm not hanging 'round, he told me.

The car had come to a stop. I did not move. I was looking at the street.

—Are you all right? he asked.

—I want to help, I whispered.

Jim turned to me. He looked at me for a while. His face was like stone. He did not speak. He just bit his lip. That was all. I got out of the car. I felt like everything had changed. I had just done something complex, irreversible, enormous. Jim went off. He waved goodbye, raising one finger from the steering wheel. There was quite a crowd in the waiting room. I bought my ticket for Dublin. I felt as though people were looking at me differently. As if I were strange, dodgy, or in some way suspect.

A beautiful woman was wearing a badge on the lapel of her jacket. 'Mise Éire'. It took me some time to pronounce these words correctly. 'Misha air-a'. 'I am Ireland'. In the train, my head leaning against the window, I searched for an image that would be my refuge. A scene, a character or a place, something that I could summon with my eyes closed to comfort my nights. The woman at the station was tall, long, too well-dressed. I wanted a woman of Ireland. So, in the jolting train, I imagined her, wrapped up in a rough, black, woollen blanket, forged wrinkle after wrinkle by war and the land, very old and very beautiful. I could see her standing, leaning forward, her hands open and her white hair falling over her eyes, shouting out her anger before the soldiers. It would be her. Mise Éire. My rebel Ireland, my comforter. Her eyes were a wild blue and her lips quivered. By the time I arrived in Dublin, the image was perfect. This woman would exist from then on. I did not know it yet, but for years, I would summon her. I called her to my bedside. I asked her to watch over me like a saint. For a long time her wrath remained intact. I never dared to imagine anything different. She was there, in that way, with her muted anger, like a frayed photograph constantly looked at.

Mise Éire. Just that. I was almost Ireland. A part of her. For Tyrone Meehan, for the blanketmen, for this angry woman, for my man in the round-collared shirt. In honour of them all.

∼

Jim called me on Thursday, 6 December 1979. I wrote it down, a worried question mark in my diary. A few days earlier Tyrone had been condemned to one and a half years in prison. I had to concentrate. When Jim spoke, I looked at his gestures, his lips, his eyes. I read his body as much as his words. On the telephone, Jim's voice was a foreign language, a wild, brutal accent. He asked me if I was listening carefully. I said I was. He told me to meet someone in a café on rue Saint-Lazare, opposite the station. He said I knew him to see, that it was to be today at two o'clock. He said thanks and hung up.

I was alone in my workshop. I was repairing a flat-back mandolin with a pyrographic mahogany back. I knew everything about this instrument, in all its detail. It was made of Brazilian rosewood, with mother-of-pearl fretboard inlays and edging alternating along the sides. It must have dated back to the 1950s. I read and reread the signature stuck on the inside. 'René Gérome. Luthier in Mirecourt'. René Gérome, born in 1910. Mirecourt, the town I did my apprenticeship in. I knew how to hold the mandolin, how to undress it string by string, look after the invisible crack that ran along its back. I knew all that. That was life, my life. My life of silence and wood. My life of fresh varnish, of paté and pickle sandwiches with a glass of Côtes du Rhône at lunchtime. My life as a quiet man, whose wife had left him five years ago because she dreamt of other things. Because she was lively and funny, because she chatted, because she danced, because she was dark-haired, because she found everything too cramped in my place, everything too dull and too grey. Because a Pernambuco bow didn't respond to her touch. Just because. I knew all that. But not the rest. I knew nothing of what was to come. Of the meeting one hour later near Saint-Lazare station. Of what was going to happen. Of who would be there. Of what I was going to be asked to do. I was sure that they had all felt this the first time. All of them. Even Connolly on my wall; even Jim, even Tyrone Meehan, even the bravest ones of all. 'A terrible beauty is born.'

It is a terrible fear at first. That moment when you leave the silence of an injured mandolin to go out into the street and walk, walk, walk, mouth dry with fear. That exact moment, right then, there, that dark instant when life goes down a certain road. I went out. I closed the door of my workshop. I lowered the metal shutter that protects the window. I went out into my December life. I was heading for winter. I was walking towards something other than what I knew. I was worried and alone. 'Mise Éire?' Yeah, right! Who is Ireland, here? I can't see her. Just a violin-maker with his head down, with varnish on the tips of his fingers, walking in a hurry towards the station. Just a man who is asking courage to hold out its hand to him.

∼

Before Ireland, I knew nothing of codes or mysteries. Before Ireland, I knew nothing of the shadows. In Mirecourt, each apprentice on rue Basse had a nickname. In my workshop, I got to know 'The Little', a young man who was too simple for lute-making, and 'Ten Grams', a kid who was so skinny his head was like the skull of a dead man. There was 'King's Foot', who could calculate precisely in his head right down to the last millimetre. And there was 'Cremona', who said that everything was better in Italy. After a few weeks, my master called me 'Cocksure'. He was so happy with himself that he repeated it three or four times, laughing.

We were learning how to make a violin back with white wood. The Little and King's Foot were bent over the workbench. I heard our master going past. He was holding a broken pot. I remember that smell of caramel and also something else, a scent of hot paint and golden wax polish. I turned around. I asked what he was carrying. He did not answer me.

—Varnish, Cremona replied, without raising his head.

When the master came back, I asked him how he made his varnish. I looked at him, straight in the eye, a file in my hand. He seemed astounded, I remember. I was proud of his surprise. So he called over 'Local', an old varnisher who had asked for 'Born and died in Mirecourt' to be engraved on his tombstone. He told him to explain to me how to make varnish, to keep nothing from me. The old workman had the same surprised look as my master. And then he nodded his head, smiling. That very evening, along with the foreman, Local asked me to note down the formula on a piece of paper, learn it by heart and then throw it away. I had my dark-blue apron on, which I still wear today. I was sitting on a box on the side of the street, beside our workshop. The foreman and the varnisher were standing, cigarettes in hand. It was springtime. I remember the evening light. Local spoke. He said that the recipe had to be put together in the following order. Two hundred grams of Vosges soil after rain, hollowed out into a little volcano. No stones, no grass, just the clay and the water from the sky. Two egg yolks, broken over the clod. Five grams of brick collected by fingernail from the wall of the Bourlier workshop, at the top of the town. A beaker of warm urine, pissed at midnight, standing, on a day when you had eaten fish. The urine was the secret, the difference between the pigmentation of our sinuous maple waves and those of Bourlier's, for example. Then it had to be simmered for four hours, stirring the whole time.

One Friday lunchtime, there was fish for lunch in the workshop. It was raining. Local bent over me and told me that today was the right day. That night, I collected a nice clod of soil. I hung around Bourlier's workshop for a while before scraping the wall with my nail. Then, standing, I pissed, into my cup, on the twelve strokes of midnight. Afterwards, I mixed the soil and the eggs, the brick and the piss in my lunchbox. I went to my stove and I stirred, with a file, stirred incessantly, my eyes burning with fatigue.

The next day, the master of the workshop inspected our white wood backs. King's Foot's was a little rounded, almost perfect. The line between the two joined pieces could not be felt with a fingertip. The Little had had difficulty with his corners and the rounded part that held the wooden edges. Cremona was happy with himself and unhappy with Vosgian wood. When the master reached my workbench, he saw only one piece of carved wood. The other piece was just a rectangle of wood with a mere pattern drawn on it with a pencil.

—That's it? asked my master.

I nodded my head. I showed him my lunchbox. It contained a block, as hard as a burnt stone.

—You spent more time on that than on the back?

I thought for a second. I said yes. My master sighed. He told me that what I had done was nothing. Definitely not a varnish. Just pride and muck. He told me that this recipe was a trick, a lesson for an apprentice. He said I was cocksure of myself.

—You will be Cocksure! my master laughed.

And then he banged my lunchbox against the workshop wall. The stone fell out. It took me an hour to scour the dented lunchbox. And then I went back to my white wood back.

—Just do what you have to do, my master advised.

It was later, three years later, that I timidly approached varnish again. I learnt. Just what I needed to. When things weren't going well, the master told us so. Nothing more.

—Not like that, he would say.

—How, then?

—Keep looking.

Before Ireland, a secret always had the smell of varnish. It was the only mystery in the world. In the nineteenth century, when another violin-maker would visit him, the great Jean-Baptiste Vuillaume would burn aniseed so that the smell of his mixture would give nothing away. Much later, I in turn became a varnisher. I secretly mixed linseed oil and Venice turpentine essence simmered for 200 hours. Much later again, I used Norwegian tar. Even later, I chose to apply thirteen layers of varnish on violin wood.

~

His name was Paddy. I had seen him several times in Belfast, with Jim and Tyrone. A big quiet lad who smiled occasionally. I put him up in the bedsit on the last floor of the building where my workshop was. A bed, a wardrobe, a table, a sink, toilets on the landing. He told me it was nice and warm. He was happy. We stood in the middle of the room. He smiled when he saw Connolly on my wall. And also the Proclamation of Independence by the Provisional Government of the Irish Republic. He asked me if there was much coming and going in the street, in the building. I said there wasn't. It was a small, quiet street that led onto boulevard des Batignolles. A building full of elderly people. He explained that he was going to get the keys cut. That I should never go up to the bedsit again as long as he was there. He also told me that other men would come by. Never more than two. He needed another mattress for the floor. He spoke slowly, calmly. He knew what he had to do. This room, these recommendations, these whispered words were his life, his mandolin. He also asked me if I wanted money for rent. I said I didn't. He insisted. I refused again. He asked me to show him around the area. I showed him the mail-sorting centre that takes up most of the district, the cafés, the bakery, the metro stations. He was delighted. Three stations surrounded the hideout: Rome,

Europe and Liège. The hideout. It was no longer a place I kipped in when it was too late to go home to Montmartre, but a hideout.

—What do I do now? I asked Paddy.

—Nothing, that's all. You just go about things as usual, he replied.

I never saw him again in Paris. Just once, about ten days later. A wave through the window of my workshop when he passed by on his way down the street. He was with another man, an older man I did not know. Then I met him months later, in Belfast. He gave me a quick wave from the footpath. I was proud, and disappointed at the same time. Not one word, barely a look in my direction, as though he had never seen me before. And then other Irish men and women came to the hideout. A little redhead with a funny walk who was not from around here. A tall man with a white beard who made a habit of saying hello to me, putting a finger to his temple when he passed by my window. A woman, Mary, who left a present in the room, a green scarf she had knitted for me. Two young tattooed lads who would have a drink in my local café and play the pinball machine, chatting loudly. They didn't even suspect that the keys were mine. I thought they were careless drinking there, just over the road, their accents grating against curious looks.

And I continued. Coming back to Paris after the big march in August 1980, I carried a bag of money. Jim and a Dubliner had handed it over to me the day before I left. We counted the notes together, behind the bar of a closed pub. There was 30,000 pounds sterling and 10,000 dollars inside. I took the train with it, and the plane. I kept the bag with me, as hand luggage. In Paris the meeting point was the same, in the Saint-Lazare café. Two men were sitting at a table at the back, waiting. I knew the younger one. He lived in Andytown. He had come to Jim and Cathy's several times for tea. He stayed at the table with me. The other one went to the toilets, down below. There we were, just sitting facing each other, without speaking. Then the other one came back up and everything became more relaxed. It was all right. The money was all there.

They offered me a beer, but I declined. I felt as though everyone was looking at us. Handshakes, a wink. I went back out into the street, my mind blank. I was neither proud, nor happy, nor anything. I had done what had to be done. Without knowing or asking for anything. And that was fine by me. I thought of Tyrone, of the blanketmen. I found it easier to walk around over there between patrols than to hand over money here. I found it strange that the war should spill over its borders in this way. I knew that the IRA would never target British interests on French soil. France was just a support base. A place of transit, to fall back to or to rest in. But the IRA operated in Germany, in the Netherlands, elsewhere than on their own soil. And I knew that maybe this money was helping them. And that it would help to kill. And that it would kill. And that these men who slept in my bedsit would perhaps also kill. But there you have it. That's the way things were. I had entered the terrible beauty and there was no turning back.

Interrogation of Tyrone Meehan by the IRA

16 DECEMBER 2006

It's a colour video. The image is of Tyrone Meehan, alone, worried, standing behind a table and leaning against a grey wall. He is wearing a brown tweed mottled jacket and is holding his cap in his hand. He is not looking at the camera. There are other people in the room who cannot be seen. Tyrone Meehan is speaking.

—*Am I under arrest?*
—*Sit down and calm down.*
—*I am asking you a question, Mike O'Doyle. Am I under arrest?*
—*Sit down.*
—*Answer me, Mike.*
—*We are not masked. You are looking us right in the face and you are not tied up; that should be enough of an answer for you.*
—*Then let me go.*
—*We have to question you.*
—*I said everything at the press conference.*

—We have other questions.

—I have the right to remain silent.

—You have no rights here.

—I don't know you. I am talking to Mike O'Doyle.

—What is your name?

—I am not playing at that.

—Your name?

—You know my name, Mike.

—Speak up.

—Ah for fuck's sake, I've known you for over forty years. I was around before you were born. Stop messing around, Mike.

—Give us your name. It's the procedure.

—What procedure? The IRA has laid down its arms. There is no procedure any more.

—We're in charge here. So calm down, give us your name and it will all work out all right.

—I know how it works out when you talk.

—You have nothing to fear. Your name?

—You know my name like I know yours, Mike O'Doyle.

—The IRA is asking for your name, not mine.

(Silence)

—The sooner you answer, the sooner you'll see your wife and son again.

(Silence)

—You know nothing is going to happen to you.

—I know you, Mike, but not these other two. I only want to talk to you.

—I'm telling you nothing is going to happen to you.

—Well then why are you filming all this?

—So there is a record.

—A record?

—Proof that your interrogation went all right.

—And after? What happens to me after if I answer your questions?

—*You will be able to leave.*

—*I don't believe you.*

—*You have no choice.*

—*No one ever comes out of shit like this alive.*

—*We have laid down our arms; you said it yourself.*

(Silence)

—*Will I be able to stay in Ireland?*

—*You are free.*

—*And if I refuse to answer?*

—*Relieve yourself. Talk.*

—*I'll be free?*

—*You will be free as well.*

(Long silence)

—*Your name?*

—*Meehan.*

—*Louder.*

—*Meehan.*

—*First name?*

—*Tyrone.*

—*When and where were you born, Tyrone Meehan?*

—*The eighth of March 1925 in Killybegs, Donegal.*

—*At what age did you join the IRA?*

—*I can't remember. Around seventeen. When we came to live in Belfast.*

—*You can't remember?*

—*Around seventeen, in 1942.*

—*You were imprisoned almost immediately?*

—*I was interned in February 1943. In 1957. I was done for five years in September 1971. I was imprisoned for fifteen months in October 1979 and I was briefly arrested in November 1981.*

—*Briefly?*

—*A few days.*

—*You said you have been betraying us for nearly twenty-five years. Could you be a bit more precise?*

—*Since November 1981.*

—*After the hunger strikes?*

—*Around then, yes.*

—*What do you mean, around then?*

—*Yes, after the hunger strikes.*

—*You said to us: 'I was compromised at a delicate time in my life.' What does that mean?*

—*I don't want to explain myself.*

—*You will have to.*

(Silence)

—*We need to know.*

(Silence)

—*Do you want a glass of water?*

(Silence)

—*Do you want to rest, Meehan?*

—*Yes please.*

—*We'll stop there for tonight. Switch that off.*

THE MARTYR

To Tyrone Meehan! shouted the small man on the stage. It was Saturday, 19 January 1981. Tyrone was free, back amongst us. I was standing. I raised my glass, shouting. Sheila was cheering. Jim whistled through pursed lips. Cathy banged her pint on the table. At the front, at the back, the Thomas Ashe was awash with happiness. Tyrone crossed the room quickly with his hand in the air. He got up on the stage. The musicians made space for him at the microphone.

—I'd ask you to spare a thought for our sons on the blankets. Think of them all the time, everywhere, whispered Tyrone Meehan.

He leaned forward, his hand shielding his eyes from the light.

—Come up here, Mary Flaherty! And you, Evelyn Davey! And you too, Rose Flynn! Come on up here with me!

Three white-haired women left their tables amidst the applause. One of them had her hands in the air. The others were arm in arm. Tyrone Meehan helped them climb the steps. He lined them up in front of the room, saying that these mothers' children had been living in their cells, naked, for two years. And that without them, the boys would no longer have any hope. And that without us, these mothers would not have the strength. He hugged them for a long time, tenderly, one after the other. They were smiling, thanking the crowd for its cheers. He said that it was they who should be cheered, not him. That they were the cement that kept the movement together. That their suffering was worse than what the men were enduring.

I watched Tyrone. He had got out of prison the previous day. He was just like he had been fifteen months earlier, unbroken and smiling. With his bushy eyebrows, his white hair grazing the collar of his shirt, cap in hand, his wide woollen knitted tie and his tweed jacket hanging down, a little loose. He wore the brown cord trousers that I had given him as a present as well as a pair of shoes I had bought for him on rue de Clichy. Over his heart he had pinned a golden phoenix, the symbol of Irish Republicanism.

Our table was covered with pints. Men and women came over to see us, the way one would pay a neighbour a visit. There were two empty chairs for them. They sat down, exchanged a few words, a smile, a few glances, and then left to leave room for others. I was beside Tyrone, so close I could touch him. He would put his arm around my shoulder while he laughed with others. I was finishing off a pint and had more lined up. He put his hand on my knee, squeezed it, leaned towards me and quietly asked me to follow him.

—Come with me, son.

That was all. Smiling, not looking at me, his hand on my knee. He got up. I followed him. I followed him like I did that time he taught me how to take a piss, so long ago. He walked between the tables. He responded to a wave, a nod, a quick word. He went towards the bar. He lifted up the hatch. I was still following him.

We went through to the other side, among the waiters in their black ties. He exchanged a nod with the owner of the club, a fat man called Peter, who opened a green door. Tyrone turned around and let me go in first. It was a grey, empty room. There was a table and two chairs facing each other. Tyrone sat down on one of them. With a flick of his chin, he indicated I should take the other. Peter closed the door behind us.

Tyrone looked embarrassed. He fished around in his pocket and placed a key on the table. It was the key to my room. A simple, silver key, hanging on the end of an anchor keyring. I was cold. The small room was dark. Tyrone was dark too. In fact, it no longer was Tyrone. It was Meehan. Mister Meehan. A 56-year-old Irishman who had put his cap back on. Who was lighting a cigarette, looking at me over the lighter. Who was not saying anything. Who was scaring me a little.

—What is that? asked Meehan.

—The key to my place, I said.

—Who did you give it to?

I lowered my eyes. I listened to the music pulsing outside the room, the voices, the drunken shouts, the joyful evening.

—Who to, son?

—I don't know their names.

Meehan smiled. Not a Tyrone smile. There was nothing nice, nothing friendly, nothing welcoming about it. It was just an embarrassed movement of the lips and the eyes. He pushed the key towards me and asked me to put it in my pocket. And then he stood up and leaned against the wall. He spoke in a low voice, saying each word as you recite a poem. The way you talk to a child.

—You are not Irish, whispered Tyrone Meehan.

He told me I didn't have the right. That the struggle was not and never would be mine. He told me that I was no longer to lend out my room. That I was no longer to smuggle money. That I was putting people in danger. That I was playing at war. That I was amusing myself. That no-one had the right to change histories. That this was not the International Brigades. Nor the Foreign Legion. That I was French, that I could get into politics back home, trade unionism back home, that I could get involved in the environmental struggle, or that of immigrants. That I was needed at home. That I was a friend of Ireland's, a comrade, a brother, but that here I was a bystander.

I understood everything he said to me. Every look and every word. Tyrone Meehan sat down again. He held out his hand to me. The hand of a farmer, or a labourer, a poor man or a man who has toiled hard. A damaged hand, creased with time, a hand that has worked the land and the brick. He asked me to hold out mine. To put it down flat, palm facing up, beside his. My hand that worked with varnish, rosin and wood.

—Promise me you'll drop all that, asked Tyrone.

I didn't say anything. I looked at him.

—Never again, son. I already have one son behind bars, I don't want another one. It is not your destiny.

I felt like crying. It was unfair. I did have the right. I was from here, like him, like Sheila, like Jim, like all the others. I had joined the ranks of the Republic. No one could prevent me. No one. Not even my big man in the round-collared shirt. I would fight on my own, in my corner, without telling anyone a thing.

—Promise me.

—I promise you, I answered Mister Meehan.

He looked at me for a long time.

—All right then, I believe you.

He bent over the table and took my face in his hands.

—You wee insignificant volunteer.

And then he got up. He knocked on the door. Peter opened it. We had been locked in. Tyrone hugged me. He brought me to the foot of the stage where the band was finishing 'Danny Boy'. During the applause, he made me go up the steps. The musicians moved over. I had never seen the room from here. At the back, at the round table, near the big turf fire in the hearth, Jim and Cathy were talking to other people. It was late. Half the men and women were stumbling from one chair to another. Tyrone Meehan removed his cap and took the microphone. He was still holding me by the shoulder. Silence took hold. Not right away, but here and there, as from one end of the room to the other voices called for silence.

—Quiet, please!

Tyrone Meehan spoke. He said that people here had surely seen me before. That they had passed by me without really knowing who I was. And that today they had to know. I was called Antoine, I was French, Parisian and a violin-maker. While the British inflicted torture and death on her, I offered Ireland her most beautiful music. He said that I closed my eyes when I played. That my violin became anger. And that was the way I was. That was my fight. And my beauty. And my courage. And my value. That everyone had to help Ireland in his own way. There were mothers, at the back of the room, who were trembling for their children. There were volunteers, fighters, soldiers whose hands burned from the guns they wished they could lay down. There were others, all those ordinary people who demonstrated incessantly to support the struggle, who suffered in silence or by shouting. And that there were the others, all the others, those without whom there would be nothing. Friends, those who lived far away, the brothers of hope. Those three Americans, over there by the door! Yes, you over there! You who have come from Boston to support us and who we thank from the bottom of our hearts. There was a French violin-maker who offered his discreet presence as a pledge of solidarity. And that they had to be applauded, all of them, loudly. And encouraged, all of them, patiently. Because the struggle had only just begun.

We got down off the stage. The whole way to our table, I touched a hundred hands. Tyrone Meehan was still holding me by the shoulder. He laughed with one and all.

—Promise me! he shouted in my ear in the middle of the hubbub.

—I promise you, I repeated, looking at him.

At the table, Jim gave us the thumbs-up. Cathy kissed me. Sheila held Tyrone's pint out to him. It had gone flat. The creamy head was yellow. He took it, went to the hearth, plunged the poker into the embers and then into the black liquid. It rose, hissing. The foam surged to the brim. Tyrone lifted his glass, looked at it, looked at me and put his hat back on as he drank.

~

On 1 March 1981, I heard that Bobby Sands was starting a hunger strike in an attempt to obtain political prisoner status. I was in Paris. I read about it in a creased newspaper, forgotten on a café table. The article got it all wrong. The facts, the dates, the places, the terms were all wrong. The IRA was referred to as the Irish *Revolutionary* Army. Long Kesh prison was described as a 'prison for Catholic extremists'. The hunger strike was analysed as 'suicide blackmail organized by Republican warmongers'. I had never seen Bobby Sands. When I arrived in Ireland, he was already a prisoner. That previous winter, a first hunger strike had been unsuccessful. Margaret Thatcher had promised a gesture of humanity if the strike ceased. As soon as it ended, the British Prime Minister went back on her word and pursed her lips, saying she would never give in.

I was there, just sitting at a table facing out onto the street. I had folded the newspaper and was looking at my Parisian neighbourhood, the sky-grey buildings. A passer-by laughed with his girlfriend, who was gesticulating in the middle of the footpath. The noise of the coffee machine. The clinking of glasses. The green saucer and my French change. I felt far away, lost and lonely. I had known that a second hunger strike would start in the spring. Jim, Tyrone, they had all explained it to me. Through this fasting to the death, Republican prisoners would end five years of protest that had led to nothing.

Bobby Sands was the Officer Commanding of the IRA in Long Kesh, condemned to fourteen years for possession of arms. He would lead the Movement. One week later, another would join him. Then a third. And then a fourth. And a fifth would replace the first one to die. And a sixth would take the place of the second martyr. The list of volunteers drawn up inside the prison had dozens of names on it, then hundreds. Bobby Sands' smiling face joined the letter H on every brick of the city.

I didn't go to Belfast for two months. I didn't dare. I hid. Jim filled me in. Tyrone sent me posters and stickers. Bobby Sands had joined Connolly and Yeats on my workshop wall. I was seething. One evening, I walked out of a meal with friends because someone made fun of the hunger strike. He said that losing a bit of weight was good for your health. That it was just stupid. I lost it. I shouted that he didn't know a thing about it, that he was talking about things that were bigger than him, me and all of us around this table. The guy said he had had enough. That all I ever talked about was that. All the bloody time. Non-stop about Northern Ireland, spouting off about it, spiralling out of control. That I didn't even realize it, that I was pissing everyone off with this bullshit. That

I had changed. That I didn't listen to anyone. That I had lost my sense of humour. That I always looked glum. That I was ridiculous with my worried expressions, my music with my eyes closed, my air of conspiracy, my Republican badges in the winter and my Republican jerseys in the summer. That I was a monomaniac. That I was mad.

I got up. No one defended me. Not one fraternal word. My friends did not dare lift their eyes. I insulted them in English, standing up, bending over, my hands flat on the table. The guy shrugged his shoulders, shaking his head. One girl hid a laugh in her hand. I knocked over my chair and left. I slammed the door. I walked in the April night with my fists clenched. I no longer belonged here, this place with buildings that block out the sky. This place meant nothing to me. I wanted Tyrone Meehan, Jim, the look on their faces, the Falls Road, Bobby Sands' smile, the smell of turf in the hearth, winks at the corners of streets, a hand on my shoulder, the jolt of black taxis, the children in school uniform, chips leaving grease stains on newspaper, my pint of the black stuff, the metal of the enemy armoured jeeps, the bitter sound of fifes, the dull sound of drums, the sky over Ireland, its rain, its skin. I had heard that in Long Kesh, morning, noon and night, prison guards brought a meal tray to Bobby. They set it down beside him. They acted as if nothing was wrong. They were certain that this ceremonial would break him. They were waiting for him to give up. For weeks even the smell of food distressed me.

I walked for a long time. I crossed streets, hugged the walls with my head down, barely breathing. I had eaten too much, drunk too much. The girl's laughter kept coming back, the guy's gestures, the others' silence. I decided to spurn them.

On boulevard de Sébastopol, a man had built a cardboard shelter. Four walls, a corrugated iron roof. Placards were hung up all around. He explained that he was a shopkeeper and that he was closing his shirt shop because of tax he owed the Inland Revenue. To make himself heard, the shopkeeper had begun a hunger strike. The number 4 was drawn in blue chalk on a slate. This was the fourth day. He was at the door of his shelter, lying on a camp bed, a bottle of water set down beside a cup of sugar.

I looked at him. His hair was flat, he had stubble, bags under his eyes and slack skin. I couldn't accept him, I believed neither his anger nor his pain. He was listening to the radio. A woman was crouching down beside him, talking to him. They were laughing about something I was not privy to. And then he noticed me. He was worried by me. By my eyes. He smiled uncomfortably when I approached him. He was afraid. I violently pulled off the placards. I kicked the cardboard boxes. I was shouting. I screamed at the shopkeeper that he was not going to die. That he would never have the courage to die. That I was ashamed for him. That he was soiling the struggle of other men. I was crying. I knocked over his bottle of water. The woman left, walking backwards. The man got up and ran across the road. I found myself in the middle of the mess, amidst the trampled boxes, the upturned bed, the scattered tracts. I was waiting for something or someone to fight. I had no idea I harboured such hatred. From the other side of the road, a couple was staring. I was bent over, legs spread, fists clenched, gob open, panting like a dog. A young man looked away as he passed. Cars drove by.

Never. I would never again accept that a man mimic a hunger strike. Let him do it when the injustice he faces is fatal, and he has tried everything and no longer has any choice. And let him therefore suffer, day after day, let his lips bleed, his skin peel, his bones stick out, his tears dry up and his eyes close. Let him do it until he triumphs or until he dies. If not, he should stay silent. He should not dare. Ever. I was there, in the street, in the utter silence, lost, forgotten in the wood, angry tears streaming. I wiped my face with a swipe of my sleeve. And that was it. I went home.

~

I do not know why I knelt down. I am a Catholic by name, by default. Because there is no fear in heaven. I do not go to Mass, I remember neither the songs nor the prayers. But that day, on the Falls Road, in the early morning, I fell to my knees. A shout had woken me up. I was sleeping in Jack's bed, at Tyrone and Sheila's, because Jim and Cathy were in Dublin. It was four o'clock in the morning on 5 May 1981. A man screamed in the street. I do not know if it was a drunken or an angry cry. It was a heart-wrenching scream telling us that Bobby was dead. That was all. 'Bobby is dead!', repeated over and over in a voice marked by smoke and beer. Tyrone was barechested in the living room. He had turned on his radio. He was buttoning a shirt. Sheila came down in her nightdress and shawl, her bare feet in slippers. She went out into the street, rosary beads in hand. All around, the grating noise of bin lids being banged against the ground. At their windows, women were banging the bottom of saucepans with ladles or spoons.

—Bobby is dead, whispered Tyrone, putting on his cap.

He had known Bobby Sands in prison. Jim too had been with him in the cages of Long Kesh. I went outside. The whole west of the city was crashing metal. Sheila did not go very far. She stood at the corner of the Falls Road. Kneeling down with dozens of women, her head bowed. Kids were in pyjamas, their hands full of stones. Helicopters swept their white floodlights over the rooftops. Never in my life had I seen so many tears. Men were hitting walls with their bare fists. Mothers had taken children out of their cots. Daughters, sons, fathers and elderly people walked aimlessly in the middle of the dead streets. There were no British. Not one armoured jeep, not one patrol. Farther up, stones were hitting the wire fence around the army barracks. A man tore off his black woollen jumper to make a flag. He raised it in front of his window. I stayed with Sheila. I knelt down. She was saying her rosary. Beside her, the women were praying. Some men came over to join us. Young lads knelt down in the middle of the street. The sound of stones thrown into the void, metal being banged against the footpath, screams, whispered prayers, lamentations.

—No violence! No violence!

IRA men, in plain clothes and without weapons, were going around the streets with their arms in the air, calling for calm. They asked everyone to go home. To avoid provocation. To prevent other deaths. Tyrone joined them. He made a young Catholic discard his petrol bomb against a wall. He roughly frisked another who was running towards the British barracks.

—Bobby will be avenged! Be dignified! Tyrone Meehan was shouting.

It was six o'clock in the morning. All the front doors were open. Everyone was going in and out of each other's homes. The street smelt of tea. Two IRA volunteers appeared at a corner. Armed with rifles. Scarves over their mouths and black berets.

—Defend your people! shouted an old man.

The Republicans walked in the shadows along the brick walls, their arms in the air.

—All right, Pete! one of the women said on her doorstep.

—Hiya Trish, replied one of the volunteers.

I tried to remember the 'Our Father'. The words came back. 'Hallowed be thy name.' I closed my eyes. Bobby Sands was dead. This was momentous news. A hunger striker, he had been elected as an MP at Westminster by the nationalists of Fermanagh/South Tyrone. He was locked up, but also a British Member of Parliament. He had played along. The Republican people had gone to the booths to give him a voice. When his election was announced, at the height of his agony, Ireland surged. Thatcher could never, ever, let a member of her parliament die of hunger. Never. 'Thy will be done on earth as it is in Heaven.' And then he did die. After sixty-six days. And Francis Hughes was going to die in turn, and Ray McCreesh, and Patsy O'Hara. If they had let Bobby Sands die, the others did not have the slightest chance. 'Deliver us from evil. Amen.'

Tyrone Meehan crouched down beside me. A light rain was falling. He told me the tea was ready. That I was going to get cold. That I should go inside. The city was black. It was a tomb. An injured animal. Utter distress. I followed him in. I was barefoot, in my pyjamas, and wet. I went up to the bedroom and took my violin. I went back out into the street. I sat down on the footpath like a kid. I played 'The Foggy Dew'. Slowly, for me, for Bobby, for my part of the street. A neighbour set a scalding cup of milky tea on the ground. Two children sat on either side of me. I played like I never would again. In a theatre made for the occasion. Under the orange of the lamp posts, protected by a curtain of rain, by the men's anger and the women's prayers and these two children.

In the morning, at Westminster, in front of a silent assembly, a spokesperson for the British government announced that 'Mister Robert Sands' had died during the night.

Jim came back from Dublin immediately. Cathy stayed on with her parents. The day before the funeral, Jim asked me if I wanted to pay my last respects. I said I did. A young woman came to get us in a car. We stopped a distance from the house. We had to walk. Men were on the lookout in the area, in small groups, their hands in their pockets. A black ribbon had been tied to the door. Jim did not say anything to me. He put his hand on my shoulder, knocked twice and pushed the door open.

Bobby was there. Right there. I thought there would be a hall, a room, another room, infinitely more time to prepare myself. But he was there. In his open coffin, in a white satin shroud. Hands joined, waxen face, all powdered and made up to look alive, cotton wool in his cheeks. His bones were sticking out. He was translucent. His face was not the same as the one in the well-known photo. I could not look at him. The flag of the Irish Republic, his soldier's beret and gloves, were placed on his hollow chest. Between his fingers, the golden crucifix sent by the Pope. A Republican was on watch, in parade uniform and without a weapon, on either side of the coffin. When they were replaced, they went and got changed, dressed like us, in the upstairs bedroom.

Friends, relatives, men, women, blessed themselves in front of him. They were subdued; they spoke in a dignified way. Everything was whispered. Sometimes a young man would stand to attention. Another would salute the body, head held high. On the table were sandwiches and drinks. Tyrone was in the kitchen with two men I didn't know. He looked at me without saying a word. He just nodded his head. He seemed pleased that I was there.

I stayed for an hour. I looked at the coffin; I looked at the living. They were heartbroken and relieved as well. The agony was over. The suffering was eased. Bobby Sands was free. I looked at his mother. Her warm eagerness to welcome her guests. There were no tears. I forbade mine from falling. I kept moving my eyes from Bobby's face to Tyrone's.

The crowd never ceased, slowly walking in and out; an old woman in a black headscarf, two young boys, a priest and three friends. Eyes were lowered. I was no longer proud of anything. Not even of being here, the only foreigner in the heart of sadness.

A COFFIN ON MY SHOULDER

They died one after the other. Ten young men, between 5 May and 20 August 1981. After Bobby Sands, it was the turn of Francis Hughes, then Raymond McCreesh, Patsy O'Hara, Joe McDonnell, Martin Hurson, Kieran Doherty, Kevin Lynch, Thomas McElwee, and then Micky Devine. The hardiest died after seventy-three days of fasting. The weakest after forty-six days. The oldest was thirty years old. The youngest, barely twenty-three.

~

On 6 November 1981 Jim O'Leary died too. Cathy's husband. My Jim. Killed by the explosion of a bomb he was making, on the first floor of a tumbledown house at the bottom of the Falls Road. Two other Irish volunteers went with him. The milkman who delivered bottles to front doorsteps in the morning and a young lad from Bombay Street, with whom I used to play snooker. I was back in

Paris. It was Tyrone who phoned me. He didn't take any precautions. He told me that Jim was dead. That the British were keeping his body but that the funeral would take place early next week, probably on the Tuesday. I closed up my workshop. I took a plane to Dublin, then the train to Belfast. I was like stone. I did not speak a word. I answered no one, looked at no one. I didn't cry once. Sheila came to get me at the station. Just a hug, no superfluous words or tears. In front of Cathy and Jim's house there were several hundred people. The RUC and the British army surrounded it.

—It's been like this since yesterday, Sheila said.

The coffin was closed, resting on trestles in the little living room. The IRA had draped it in the national colours, and placed the beret and gloves on top. I hardly recognized Cathy. She was subdued and terse. She hugged me for a long time. Her ankle boots were on the living-room table. She was rubbing shiny black paint on them, smoothing over the scratches on the leather heel. Tyrone came out of the kitchen with a glass of milk. He took me in his arms. I still had my bag in my hand. I had come from Paris. I had come from peace. Five hours ago, I had been a hundred miles away. As I was closing my workshop, I heard a couple shouting at each other on the street.

—You'll always be a stupid bitch! the man was saying.

—You don't have to live with me! the woman replied.

I detested them. I despised these people, their scorn for each other, this street, these stone buildings, this cold sun. Jim O'Leary had died in Ireland. Jim O'Leary had been putting together a bomb. Jim O'Leary had been at war. And here were these two insulting each other in the middle of the road. These two who had never gone without their daily bread. I felt like I was going to throw up. Tyrone brought me out back; helped me out of the house. I vomited against the wall, my throat and eyes burning, to the deafening noise of helicopters and the crowds shouting at the soldiers.

In the early afternoon, for the second time in two days, the Republicans tried to bring the coffin out of the house. The men were in front, the women behind, some with hurleys. Nationalists had come from everywhere to lend a hand. As soon as the coffin appeared over their heads, covered in the flag, on the front doorstep, the riot police charged at the crowd. I was brutally knocked to the ground, then pushed up against the low wall of the front garden. Two children were lying beside me. The police were shoving the Catholics back with truncheons. Screams. Shots. The smell of gunpowder. Plastic bullets, fired from a few metres away at the first row of bare fists. In the midst of the scramble, the coffin overturned. It slipped off their shoulders. It fell onto the grass in front of the house. Hundreds of men ran at the police. I ran with them, I shouted with them. I had to push on people's backs with my two hands to breathe. I saw Tyrone, to my right, kicking a plexiglass riot shield. He took a blow to the brow. He was bleeding. Others were bleeding. A stone hit me on the head. I bit my tongue. I spat on the ground. I was bleeding too.

The coffin went back into the house, passed overhead from hand to hand. The Brits immediately loosened their stranglehold. The Republicans moved back. Young people were arriving from neighbourhoods all around. They jumped from wall to wall to reach Cathy and Jim's house.

—Everybody sit down! shouted Tyrone.

The crowd sat down where it was. In front of the house, in the garden, on the footpaths, in the middle of the road. I remained standing for a second. There were several hundred of us. Some old, some young. There was no fear. There was anger. The policemen had regrouped further up, at the crossroads. Army jeeps were ready and waiting. I went into the house. Jim's mother was there.

She was talking to Cathy and Tyrone in the kitchen. Tyrone looked annoyed. He shrugged his shoulders. He smiled. He held Cathy by the shoulders and said it was agreed. Then two young men folded up the Republican flag, removed the beret and the gloves from the top of the coffin and slipped them into their jackets. A priest was there. He said that it was a wise solution. That the family had to be considered. Tyrone went into the street. He asked me to follow. He was walking quickly. I followed unknowingly. My tongue was painful. He was holding a wad to his bloody forehead. We walked towards the police. Two officers moved away from the others. Tyrone told them the coffin was bare. That the flag and gloves had been removed. One policeman replied that at the slightest sign of a military funeral, in the street, on the way, in the cemetery and even after the ceremony, his men would intervene. He said that he was holding Meehan personally responsible. Tyrone spat on the ground. He threw his soiled cloth at the policeman's feet and we went back into the house.

When the coffin appeared, the crowd rose in silence. The priest walked in front. Two women and four men bore Jim's body along. Cathy and his sister first. Then Tyrone and other familiar faces. Three bearers on either side. The crowd parted. People blessed themselves in silence. There was no other noise apart from that of feet scraping along the ground. After a few dozen yards, the six bearers were replaced. And then others further on. And still others after that. Tyrone was looking for me. Without a word, he took me by the arm and placed me behind the next bearers. Cathy was crying, her head bowed. She was holding a framed photo of Jim and Denis, their son, in her arms. Sheila was crying. I think I was crying too.

At a signal, we took over from the others. I fitted the bottom of the coffin between my left shoulder and my ear, my cheek pressed against the grooves of the wood. I was the middle bearer. On my right shoulder, I felt the firm hand of the carrier on the other side. He was clasping me the way you do when you protect someone. My left arm was held out towards him horizontally, under this morbid weight, and my fingers, right at the end, pressed down on his shoulder. With my right hand, I gripped the finely wrought brass handle that stuck out in front of my face. So this was what a man-carried coffin was like. My neck was in pain and my legs were trembling. 'The coffin was carried by hand': I had read these words so many times without realizing the true meaning of them. I walked with my eyes closed. I spoke to Jim through the cold wood. I told him that I loved him. I thanked him for having brought me to him, to his country, to so many wounded hearts. A man took my place. I slipped back into the cortège. Tyrone put his hand on my shoulder. He stayed like that, leaning heavily on me, right up to the cemetery. Behind the gates, on the hills that surround Milltown, the police and soldiers kept a close eye on our grieving. Hidden by the crowd, a man offered the folded flag, the beret and the gloves to Cathy. She refused, shaking her head. She was crying, the photo of her child and her man held tightly against her heart. Jim's mother received the symbols of the dead volunteer.

At dusk, much later, when the streets were deserted, a unit of volunteers visited Jim O'Leary's grave. Four men, in marching uniform, with tricolour armbands, scarves over their mouths, armed with assault rifles. Just as they had done for Bobby Sands, they fired three honorary shots over the fresh grave. On 29 November Tyrone was arrested. He was accused of having organized the military homage to Jim. The Brits broke through the door with sledgehammers. I had gone back to Paris. Sheila told me about it. They were asleep. Tyrone opened the window to shout for help. He thought it was a Loyalist attack. And then he saw the jeeps blocking the street. So he came downstairs in his pyjamas to open the gate on the ground floor. The soldiers overturned the sofa and the bookshelves. They opened the drawers, the oven, the fridge. They searched the wardrobe, the beds, the bathroom. They took Tyrone away, barefoot and in his nightclothes. For five days they kept him in Castlereagh Holding Centre. And then they let him go, just like that. Without an explanation and without charge. They just let him go.

~

In the spring of 1982 Tyrone bought me a cap. The same as his, a wide one from Shandon's, brown herringbone tweed with a button on the top. But before that he brought me to Milltown to put some flowers on Jim's grave. His resting place was simple. A Celtic cross, a gravestone, some granite. I put my wreath in the middle of the older flowers and the faded tricolour ribbons. Tyrone was behind me, standing back from the grave. He watched me, hands in his pockets. On the right, farther away, in the middle of the brambles, the weeds and the bent headstones, a woman was sweeping a grave. Behind her, near a grey vault, a mother and child were setting a fallen vase upright. Mist hung over the hills that surround the city. My heart was cold. I read what was left of my friend. Golden letters on a black marble tablet. It was raining, just a little.

Vol. Jim O'Leary
1937–1981
2nd bat
Belfast Brigade Óglaigh na hÉireann
Killed in action
R.I.P.

I wanted to pray. I realized that I no longer knew how. I simply imagined that he was there, sitting down on the stone with one knee clasped in his hands. I whispered for him. To you, Jim O'Leary, who died at fourty-four years of age on 6 November 1981. To you, volunteer of the Belfast Brigade of the Irish Republican Army, who died in active service. To you, my friend. To you, the big lad in the rain, who advised me to open my violin case one Sunday in April 1975, before welcoming a lost Frenchman into your house. To you, the elegant man who never spoke to me about your fight. Never. Who kept silent about your way of making war.

I looked up at the sky. It looked turbulent, too big, all out of storms. It was raining even harder. When I went back over to Tyrone, he took off his cap and put it on my head, smiling.

—You need one of these, he said.

I stayed in his house from then on. In Jack's bedroom. After Jim's death, Cathy had left Belfast. She went back to live in Dublin, at her parents' house. She could no longer abide anything to do with the war. Anything to do with violence, suffering and symbols. She could no longer bear to hear her husband's name cheered in the clubs. She was like a tired, old, grey woman. She had lost her husband and her son. She was hurt. She was defeated. I was told she drank. I do not know if she is still alive. I never saw her again.

Tyrone Meehan had organized everything. Him and me, just us. A two-man tent, sleeping bags, a gas heater, a borrowed car and two raincoats. We left Belfast in the morning. The sky to the west was full and heavy. There were no enemy patrols, no jeeps. We drove along Lough Foyle and passed through Derry before going over the border into Donegal, his homeland. He whistled away to himself as he drove. I looked at Ireland through the window. The grey sea. I was moved and proud. It was a trip for no real reason. We were just returning to his birthplace to buy me a cap.

—You'll have to break it in, otherwise it'll look rare, said Tyrone.

He let go of the wheel to show me the edge of the peak that he wore low over his eyes.

—You see?

I said I did. I thought it didn't really matter. I felt good. He was still whistling away. I was looking at the moors, the blue-stained sheep, the turf bogs, the clouds hanging low. On the radio was the news of a British patrol that had been targeted in the Catholic ghetto of Ardoyne; nobody had been injured. Tyrone turned it down. He opened his window.

—Can you smell that?

—What?

—Our country.

It was the heavy, damp, threatening, earthy smell of sodden skies and ocean wrath. I looked at Tyrone. He was looking in his rear-view mirror.

—Are you all right? I asked.

—Don't I look it?

We pitched the tent near a lake, very close to the road. Tyrone had brought some brown bread, sausages and cooked cabbage. We turned in early. He had a flask of poteen – burning, sickening, made from potato peel tortured in a still. We drank it between us. Tyrone talked. He brought the flask to his lips, shook his head, closed his eyes and winced, and then talked some more. He told me he resented the British, that he felt an endless anger for their war.

—But make no mistake about it, Tyrone Meehan told me. I don't hate them because they are fighting against us. Fighting against us is nothing. It's war. They put us in prison, they torture our men, they kill us, but that is not why I resent them.

I drank from the bottle. A burning feeling ran down my insides. Tyrone lay on his back, hands clasped behind his neck, covered by a knitted woollen blanket. He had switched on a torch that lit up the tent's blue. I was lying on my side. I looked at him. He spoke in a low voice.

——I resent those bastards for what they have turned us into. I resent them because they have forced us to cheat, lie and kill. I hate the man they have made me be.

I slept on his right side, fully dressed, a little drunk, my face squashed up against the canvas. In the morning the rain woke me with its icy spattering. Tyrone wasn't there. My head was heavy, my mouth dry. I opened the tent. He was standing, his back to me, facing the black lake. The mist was breaking off towards the west and the sky was uncertain.

——All right, son? said Tyrone.

My traitor had heard the zip. He didn't look at me. He reached out his arm to grab my shoulder. I came to him. He was smoking. He hugged me like a brother. Just like he would when I wasn't feeling so good. When I was afraid, when I had doubts about everything, when at times I thought the war was useless or lost. We were standing like that, both of us, facing the lake, in the middle of his Ireland and under his sky. He didn't say anything at first. He let the wind, the light, brush over the hills and the low stone walls. His hand heavy on my shoulder, his eyes closed. I looked at him. I was proud. Of his trust most of all.

∼

After Jim's death, little by little, Tyrone had come to accept the idea that I would help the Republican struggle. That I would make my bedsit available, as I had done in the past. But for him this time, and him only.

——There's only me, do you hear me? No one else but me, Tyrone had warned. Everyone else stays out, all of them. Those are the rules of undercover work.

When he came to France, he would say he was going to Dublin or Cork. Even Sheila thought he was in Ireland. In Paris, Tyrone was never accompanied by anyone. He refused to let me come and get him from the airport. We were not to be seen together, that was the protocol. He would make his own way and meet up with me at night in my workshop. I would give him the keys of the bedsit and he would slip them into my letterbox two days later. Like the others used to do, before they were arrested. Because they had all been arrested. In December 1982, Paddy, who had been counting money in the toilets, was arrested at Roissy airport by French police, along with Mary, the woman with the scarf. The small redhead with the funny walk, who had taken the bedsit after him, was arrested in Rosslare by the Irish Special Branch as he got off the ferry. The big man with the white beard who would wave at me through the window was called John McAnulty. He was intercepted at Saint-Lazare station, along with the two tattooed young lads who had played on the pinball machine in my local café. They had been heading to Le Havre by train with false passports.

—We are not playing at war, we're *at* war, Tyrone used to say.

He did not drink in the cafés. He made no sign through the window. He did not hang around my street. He crossed roads at the green light and on zebra crossings. He took the keys and gave them back. We never spoke of what he did in France. I could only imagine. He visited escaped prisoners, he oversaw weapons transfers, he looked after the manufacture of fake ID, he transported money. I feared for him. When I saw Tyrone in Belfast, his trip to Paris had never existed. And that was it. That was my role. A miniscule involvement. Tyrone Meehan had decided it would be this way. He never asked me for anything other than my key.

I looked at my traitor. He looked out over the lake, and spoke. He said that if one day I had any doubts, if I wondered why all the violence, why all the sacrifices, why the war, why James Connolly, why Bobby Sands, why Jim O'Leary, I had to remember this silence. Wherever I was. In Belfast, in Paris, in my workshop, among friends, alone, sad, happy, in autumn or in spring. I had to close my eyes and remember this beauty. And just like that, he said, I would feel his hand on my shoulder and everything would be simple. He said I would realize then that it is fair and normal and right that men should fight for this land. I did not tell him about my dream of my old mother Ireland, of Mise Éire, of her grey hair and her white anger in the face of soldiers. She who whispered to me at night when I would lose faith.

Tyrone chose the cap for me. He brought me to a tiny shop, hidden behind a rock. The saleswoman called him by his name. He said I was like a son to him. He put a tape measure around my head, lifted up a pile of tweed.

—Try this one, said Tyrone Meehan.

It was a big cap, with a button on the top, brown and black herringbone. In the mirror, an Irishman was laughing. It was just right. Tyrone paid. I was embarrassed. He was unemployed. Sheila was a nurse. They found it hard to make ends meet. I often bought them meat so they could forget the potatoes and cabbage. On the front step of the shop Tyrone took my hat and broke it in by folding it in the middle and making the edges meet.

—Show me, the Irishman said.

I turned to face him; my hands in my pockets, my jacket a little tight, my trousers flapping around my ankles, the peak rounded, the cap tilted to the right. He looked at me and put his thumbs up.

—You were Antoine, and now you are Tony, laughed Tyrone.

And I laughed too.

THE CEASEFIRE

I really believed in peace for the first time on Monday, 22 August 1994. I was in Paris. The city already had that veiled September look about it. There was a cold, light rain. After a trip to Belfast at the beginning of the month, I had taken a few days off to visit some relatives in the Mayenne area. I had also gone to visit a friend in Mirecourt, an old violin-maker propelled into retirement by his shaking hands.

I was happy to be back in my workshop, tidying up the workbench, whistling. When the telephone rang, I looked at it without making a move. It was as if I knew. For weeks, rumours of this incredible news had been all over Ireland. The IRA had decided to lay down its arms. Not give them up, like the newspapers were writing. To whom could the IRA possibly give up its weapons? It was neither defeated nor drained of energy. This was not about military surrender but about political courage. What the IRA was offering was to lay down its arms, destroy them, accept the decommissioning of its arsenal under the observation of an independent international commission. In exchange, Sinn Féin – its political wing – would be taken on board the peace process. Protestants, Unionists, Loyalists, Orangemen, would all have to accept power-sharing with the Catholic minority. It was time for concessions.

—Tony? It's Tyrone. It's done, Tony. It's going to be announced on Wednesday night. Are you coming?

I burst into tears. I held on tight to my telephone with both hands and wept. It was done. The truce, the ceasefire, it didn't really matter what names others would give to it. It was done. Was I coming? You're damn right I was coming. I threw a few shirts and my cap in a bag and took the first flight to Dublin. I shook all the way to Belfast. I trembled like a young man in the face of happiness. Tyrone and Sheila were at the station. I ran along the platform towards them, my bag on my shoulder. I had never run like that towards anyone. Towards the doors of the station, towards the city, towards its scent of turf and damp. I laughed as I ran. Sheila, then Tyrone, then Sheila again, then all three of us knotted together, fiercely embracing in the middle of the station while people looked on, amused. And then I stood back. I took Tyrone in my arms and looked at him, my brow almost touching his.

—It's done? It's definite?

—Tomorrow at midnight, replied Tyrone. The complete cessation of military operations.

—That's what the statement says? A complete cessation?

Tyrone nodded, smiling. He took me by the shoulder, he on my left, Sheila on my right, and we went home.

Just before midnight on Wednesday, 31 August 1994, we went out into the street. Tyrone had put on a white shirt and a green woollen tie. Sheila had spent the evening putting her hair in curlers. It was like we were going out for the night. The street was full of silent families. Kids perched on walls. Elderly women chatted calmly. An armoured jeep drove past, then another, and another. Not one stone was thrown; no one shouted. Even the helicopters seemed superfluous.

—Midnight! shouted Tyrone, raising his fist.
—IRA! IRA! IRA! chanted the crowd.

Car horns were beeping. Young people were clapping and singing. A woman blessed herself as a priest went past, observing this outpouring humanity as though he had just rediscovered it.

I looked at Tyrone. There was something like a worried smile in his eyes. He told me that there was a long way to go, but that we had just done the hardest part. Walking up the road, I looked at the men's faces. Some were deadpan. The ceasefire had been decided by the IRA Army Council. And by it alone. Contrary to military rules, no assembly had been convened by the leadership to vote on the cessation of military combat. The rank and file had heard the news outside of their units. Sinn Féin politicians were convinced that the time had come to end the armed struggle. The IRA had decided to act quickly. To ignore procedure. Their deadpan faces spoke of scepticism. For days, Tyrone met many of these volunteers. Some were tempted by dissidence. He brought them back into the fold one after the other, reminding them that the ceasefire was an order and that they were soldiers.

The next day Republican Belfast draped itself in the national colours. We joined a cavalcade of cars that was going down the Falls Road, horns blaring. Sheila was driving. Tyrone had his head and torso out the window. He called to some, then others, waving at the crowd with his cap in his hand. I was in the back, waving my flag out of the window. I was singing the 'Marseillaise', laughing. In front of us was a coal lorry. Tyrone got out of the car, telling me to follow. He went over to the lorry. He jumped up onto the wooden tailgate, helped by a few kids who were on it. I got up too, gripping the outstretched hands. Tyrone was standing up, his fists on his hips. He looked as though he was contemplating his city, his people, his humble struggle. I was beside him, waving my big flag like someone declaring a parade open. Cars followed each other slowly. Each footpath, each open door, each window was full of waving hands. Beside me, a young man was looking at my friend. He asked me if that was Tyrone Meehan, the great, famous man, the ex-prisoner. I said it was him all right. The young Republican held out his hand to me. I took it. We congratulated ourselves on being here, with him, on this day that was the start of everything.

Interrogation of Tyrone Meehan by the IRA

17 DECEMBER 2006

—How long have you been betraying us, Tyrone?

—Since 1981.

—When exactly?

—The end of November, when was I arrested again.

—Were you afraid of going back to prison?

—I was tired.

—Speak up.

—I was tired.

—Tired of what?

(Silence)

—We don't force anyone to fight, Tyrone. You didn't have to betray us to give it up.

(Silence)

—Why did you do it?

—Pressure.

—Did the Brits blackmail you?

(Silence)

—*Did they have something on you?*

—*Something like that.*

—*Explain yourself.*

—*I can't.*

—*You'd better.*

—*What information did you give them, Meehan?*

—*I don't know you.*

—*Answer the question.*

—*Do you want me to ask you the question again myself, Tyrone?*

—*Yes. I'd prefer if it was you, Mike.*

—*What were the Brits asking you for?*

—*Stuff about Sinn Féin.*

—*Stuff?*

—*If the party really wanted peace, that sort of thing.*

—*You were playing at being Sinn Féin spokesman? Was that it?*

(Silence)

—*Why Sinn Féin?*

—*I don't understand the question.*

—*It's the IRA the Brits were interested in, not people who stick up posters.*

—*I never talked about the IRA.*

—*Are you fucking us about, Meehan?*

—*I don't know you.*

—*Answer the question, Tyrone.*

—*What is the question?*

—*The police were paying you, the British army was paying you, MI5 was paying you. All that just for you to inform on a legal political party?*

(Silence)

—*Listen here, Meehan. It doesn't matter who I am. I am here because it's my place and you know it. You are a paid British agent. For twenty-five years, you have been working at weakening your community. That of your parents, your friends, your comrades. You've been working at knifing in the back the ones who have loved you, protected you, who looked out for you day after day. You betrayed yourself, Meehan, and we want to know why. We want to know what the enemy knows about us. We want to know what you told them. We want to know if some of our men were arrested because of you. If some of our volunteers went down because of you. That's what we want to know, Meehan.*

(Silence)

—If the Brits hadn't let you go, you'd never have admitted having worked for them, never! Do you know why your employers are letting you go? Do you know why, Meehan? Are you not wondering why they've dropped you in it? Because we've laid down our weapons, Meehan. Because the IRA is finished. Because you're no use to them any more. So they're using you to demoralize our side. They're saying to us: a traitor! You had a traitor in your ranks. Can you believe it, you fucking Irish? And this traitor, he's one of your fucking senior officers. The Northern Command was booby-trapped, lads! Tyrone Meehan! Your great Meehan! He had bugged his living room, his car! We could even hear your crap jokes and your shitty songs. All right, we'll give Meehan back to you! He's yours! Do you understand that, Meehan? That's what your employers want, and that's why we'll not touch your fucking face. Because if one bullet is shot in your direction then the whole world will be shouting about the breakdown of the ceasefire! Do you get it? The IRA killed an informer! The IRA killed one of its own men! The IRA has taken up arms again! They want you dead! They want to use your fucking dead body, but it's not going to happen! You are going to live, Meehan. You will live with your black soul and it'll be a dirty life. You are going to live because you are nothing any more, Meehan, just a traitor betrayed by a bunch of bastards.

(Silence)

—Speak, for the memory of your father, Tyrone.

—*Spare me, Mike.*
—*Do you want us to stop until tomorrow?*
—*Please.*
—*OK. That'll do.*
—*Nobody died because of me. I didn't betray in that way.*
—*Tomorrow, Meehan. We'll take this up again tomorrow.*
—*Switch off the cameras.*

MY TRAITOR

It was a winter morning last year: Friday, 15 December 2006. I was straightening an ebony fret with a plane. Two of the beaks of the violin had been knocked off. The boards were slightly damaged, as well as the edges of the belly, near the strings. The bridge was missing. The back was cracked. The D and E pegs were also missing. Augustin Chappuy had branded his name under the varnish on the nose of the neck. Originally from Mirecourt, he had worked miracles with violins. I dated the instrument to shortly before 1780. The remaining pegs were made from rosewood. The back and the neck were made from maple and the belly from spruce. A violin-maker from Saint Etienne, J.B. Portier, restored the instrument in September 1909. He had stuck his label on the inside and signed it.

I placed the instrument on a chamois cloth. I worked on it slowly. It was snowing. My eyes wandered from the black wood to the grey window. There was no hurry to repair it. I had plenty of time. I imagined the violin-maker from Saint Etienne, scalpel in hand, retracing the purfling by the dim light of a lamp. I could see him in his overalls, his untidy white hair. I stroked the violin, from the scroll to the button. I have felt this pleasure only once. A collector had brought me a superb Amari. He wasn't comfortable playing it. He wanted me to plane the curve of the neck just above the nose, so that it would support his hand better. He asked if he could stay. I said it would take some time. He sat down beside me, on the stool, and he watched my penknife cut into the wood. And I was trembling.

I did not react immediately. The radio was on low. Two Japanese passers-by were taking a photograph of my window. I heard 'Northern Ireland' and then the word 'traitor'. I turned up the sound. But the news had moved on. I put down my plane. It seemed to me that the name Tyrone Meehan had entered the room. It was just an impression. Something unpleasant was lurking there like a shadow. I had heard Tyrone's name, that was certain. I wondered why I had suddenly thought of my friend's smile as the tourist took a photo of me.

Tyrone was to come to Paris the following week. He had been travelling less since the ceasefire, but still used my place sometimes. 'Peace takes time to implement. Everything has to be cleaned up,' he said one day. Last spring he had come to stay with Sheila. It was her first visit. I brought them everywhere. Montmartre, the Eiffel Tower, along the Seine, the cafés. Tyrone was paying for most of this and I resented it. So did Sheila, who frowned at him whenever he picked up the bill. He pretended it was his first trip to Paris. He acted amazed all the time, winking at me as soon as she had her back turned.

I called Tyrone. It was Sheila who answered. Her voice was strange. She told me to call back later or some other time. She seemed anxious and in a hurry. She hung up. I called back later that evening. Jack answered. In keeping with the peace process, Meehan junior had been freed in July 2000, along with the last prisoners from Long Kesh. I liked him a lot. He called me 'wee bro'. I asked him how things were. 'Bad', was his response. He said there was a problem with Tyrone. That he had been accused of something serious but that it was all going to work out all right.

I switched the radio back on. Nothing. Northern Ireland had disappeared from the news. I went out. There was a newsstand beside the entrance to the Rome metro station. I bought an evening paper. I opened it, and I keeled over. I had unfolded the paper; I was walking along; I read a headline, a few lines and then I collapsed. Not like a fall. It was neither violent nor sudden. Quite simply, I just stopped everything. I was a few yards away from my workshop. I stopped walking, I stopped reading, I stopped holding myself up. I let myself fall. I let go of the newspaper. I sat down heavily, then lay down on my back, my head hitting the ground with a dull thud. People passed by, saying nothing, staring. Then a postman leaned over me. And a woman. A young man, too, was saying something about my having fainted. The postman sat me back up carefully. He took off his gloves. He opened the top button of my shirt. He said I looked grey. That my lips were blue. The waiter from the café came over with a glass of water. He called me 'Monsieur Antoine'. He asked if I was all right. I nodded. The newspaper was leaving me page by page, carried off by the wind.

I don't know how but I found myself back in my workshop. Sitting on the visitors' stool. I looked at the battered violin. I looked at my wall. The files, wedged by the dozen onto their wooden stands. My knives, their maple handles threaded with ebony. I looked at the gouges, the spiral peghole reamers, the purfling groove cleaners, the scissors, the planes, the clamp screws, the wedges, the cam clamps, the chisels, the sound post setters, old guitar frets forgotten in a corner of the workbench like a game of pick-up-sticks. I looked at the mess of cloths soiled by splinters of wood, shavings, dust, leftover cords wrapped around my lamp, boxes, lids, bits of sandpaper, bunches of paintbrushes in chipped cups. I looked at the jars of varnish, the bottles full of secrets, I looked at my one-ring stove, the saucepan of hardened fish glue. I looked at the rough wood, the piled-up chunks of spruce and maple, left for years to dry. For a long time, I looked at the violins hanging from the hooks like butchers' cuts. Somehow it all seemed unfamiliar. I sat staring at this mess, a sienna glow in the dusky gloom.

At a loss, I turned to my wall, to the big man with the round neck collar, and that other man with long hair, that Bobby Sands who smiled at death. I read Yeats' poem and its terrible beauty again. I looked at the Proclamation of Independence, 'In the name of God and of the dead generations ...' I was no longer breathing. My mouth was dry. I felt hollow. My head was throbbing. The snow had stopped. The street was quiet. I sat, my hands between my thighs. I was cold. Never had I been so cold. The light was out. I was a shadow, slouched, head bowed, mouth open. I could feel my heart beating. I was breathless. I put my elbows on the workbench. I put my head in my hands.

It was a very short article. One of those quickly read pieces that fill up the columns of a newspaper like a wedge under furniture. 'A traitor within the IRA', the headline stated in bold. Almost immediately, Tyrone's name appeared, right at the beginning of the line. I had never seen it written before. Not like that, not in a French newspaper with his age right beside it. 'Tyrone Meehan, 81.' The article said that this Irishman was a 'high-ranking member of the terrorist organization'. That he had admitted having betrayed the Republican movement for twenty-five years. That he had been paid for his information. That he had announced it in Dublin, at a press conference hastily called by Sinn Féin. The article also said that it was a blow to the credibility of nationalists, but that it wouldn't endanger the peace process.

I got up. I still had my coat on. My cap was hanging on the peg. I put it on, then took it off. I went out with my head bare. I walked for a long time. I felt numb. I don't think I passed anyone. Paris was totally deserted. I went as far as the Seine. I walked along the bank looking at the shades of light on the water. My lips were pursed. My jaw ached. My fists were clenched. I hated that newspaper. I hated all newspapers. These lies were killing me. These journalists with inky blood on their hands were killing me. They wrote without knowing, without thinking. Those people who repeat each other's mistakes to the point of inanity. What could he look like, the one who wrote that Tyrone Meehan was a traitor? How dare he? What did he know?

I was walking alongside the Louvre. My mobile rang. It had taken me a long time to accept this object. I only know how to type a number and flip it open to take a call. It was Jack again. He asked me how I was. He was speaking in his prisoner's voice. A hard, sharp tone. He told me to listen, and to be quiet. Not to interrupt, at all. I kept on walking. Then I stopped; I sat on a freezing bench. Jack was talking slowly. He was using easy words for his French kid brother. In six years, he had got to know me. He told me everything. First of all, that I was welcome any time in Belfast. That it was still my city, as it had always been. That I had friends there and that he was one of them and always would be. He told me that his father had betrayed them. That they didn't know anything else. He had given himself up to Sinn Féin, saying he had problems. The Republican party got him over the border and held a press conference in a Dublin hotel. Jack said that his father had admitted it publicly. He had been betraying them for twenty-five years. He was a British agent. He was paid regularly. He didn't say anything else. After the press conference, Tyrone Meehan had been taken away by the IRA to be questioned. Sheila and Jack were assured that he would be brought back to them afterwards. The British had offered Tyrone the possibility of starting afresh elsewhere, but he refused. He wanted neither a false name nor exile. He asked to remain in Ireland. That was it. Sheila was like a dead person. Jack was waiting for his father to come back to make sense of it all. Their neighbourhood was torn between hostility and compassion. In a few hours, Tyrone had become 'that bastard Meehan'. Men spat his name on the ground when leaving the Thomas Ashe. Jack said that was all. That's just the way it was. That before getting angry with him, we'd have to wait to find out more. That this was his father, but that he was a traitor too. Then he hung up.

I walked back to the workshop. It was winter inside me. I decided not to go home, but to sleep in the bedsit where Tyrone had slept. The hideout was tiny. A narrow bed, a table, a chair, an empty shelf and a rug. No trace of the people who had stayed here. I turned on the electric heating and opened the fanlight. The sink was covered in dust. A blanket, folded up at the end of the bed. I lay down, fully dressed, hands by my sides. I switched off the bedside lamp. I looked up at the florescent star that the red-haired guy had stuck onto the ceiling. I thought of the way he walked because of his shattered knee. Of John McAnulty and his white beard. Of Mary and her scarf. Of Paddy, who imitated the violin by making a funny sound with his throat. Of the two tattooed guys who challenged the pinball regulars by betting them a beer.

∼

—Promise me you'll stop all that, Tyrone had advised me.

I can still see him. In the freezing storeroom, behind the bar, while the room was still cheering him. He had asked me who I had given my key to. I had refused to answer. He knew about Paddy. He had gone to his place to get the keys back for himself. For two years he did not speak of it. In the winter of 1981 he started up again. He wanted to know who the others were, all those I had put up. He said it was for my own safety. He drove me around Belfast. He was tense. We searched for five days. The redhead with a limp was having a pint at the door of the Beehive, a pub on the Falls Road.

—Him, I said.

John McAnulty was driving a black taxi. We drove past him by chance on our way towards Whiterock. Tyrone did a U-turn and we followed the black Austin. He overtook it. I looked at the driver. His smile, his white beard.

—Him too, I said.

One of the young tattooed guys was playing snooker in the back room of a club. He was smoking and talking loudly.

—He was in Paris too, with another lad like him.

—That's Tommy, his brother, revealed Tyrone, leading me outside.

We found Mary at her weekly bingo in Short Strand.

∼

I watched the star lose some of its light. I put my hands over my mouth. The room became ice-cold. I could see Tyrone again. He had a different expression from usual. He looked at these men, one after the other. He seemed neither annoyed nor satisfied. He asked me if I had helped any others. If I was sure. That day he told me that only he was to have my key. One year later, Paddy, John, Mary, the redhead and the two brothers were arrested.

I looked at the dead star. The room was throbbing. So were my head, my blood, my rigid neck. The silence was closing over me like a vault. Tyrone had used me. One by one I had nominated good people for his prison.

I didn't sleep. I watched the darkness. In the middle of the night, the snow turned back into rain. The room filled with a city cold that drips down windows like a dirty trail. I kept my shoes and my coat on; I didn't even think of getting under the sheets. The look on Tyrone's face. His arm on my shoulder in front of the black lake. His influence. His words. I was feverish. I longed to see him. I felt an evil chill freeze my lower back, my neck, flow down the leg hanging off the bed. I lay on my back, hands clasped on my chest. My mind was blank. I just let it all wash over me. I was an open door. I heard what sounded like a moan. I was moaning. A child's whinge. I turned and lay on my side, shoulders hunched, my head falling onto my chest and my knees pulled up. I was hurting. I didn't know where. My skin burned. My fists were clenched under my chin. It was neither weakness nor anger, but withdrawal. I was drowning. I was afraid. I searched for my image of Ireland. I called up the memory of my rebellious old woman. But that night, on my shipwrecked bed, she would not come. I prayed. And then I gave up.

It was six o'clock. I got up. I went out into the street and walked. I went right up to Montmartre. I didn't recognize anything. I think I went into a café. I remember the smell of bread. I remember the noise of a bin lorry. I decided I'd never go to Belfast again. Never. Well, not right away. I couldn't. Everything frightened me. Jim was dead, Cathy was lost in grief, Tyrone was a traitor, Sheila had been betrayed. They were Belfast. Those four and no one else. I knew lots of people in Belfast. That meant no one. A wink here, a hello there, a handshake sometimes, a glance, familiar faces, but so what? Jim and Tyrone were my Irishmen. I didn't stay in Belfast,

I stayed at Jim O'Leary's. I didn't march in the streets alongside Republicans, I marched with Tyrone Meehan. It was them. That was it. My Ireland was founded on two friendships. My Ireland was built on sand. I was a Parisian violin-maker. I played the violin amidst foreign suffering. I had made up another country for myself. I was bowled over by everything. I was over.

I decided to go to Belfast after all, as soon as possible. I bought an English newspaper at a news-stand at Place de Clichy. On the front page there were two photos of Tyrone. His bushy eyebrows, his white stubble, his Donegal eyes, his smile, his soft cap, his checked shirt. The other picture had been taken in Dublin at the press conference. It was of a very old man. His head was leaning slightly to one side. He looked weary and his lips were thin. He was almost bald. He was wearing glasses I hadn't seen before. His eyes and skin were different. There was none of his light. But it was Tyrone Meehan nevertheless. I went into another café. I drank a glass of white wine, a Pomerol. Then another. I kept glancing at the paper. I wouldn't go to Belfast right away. I couldn't. But I had to. Tyrone had to talk to me. He had to explain. Jack was right. I had to see him. I didn't want to read any more, hear any more, guess any more. I wanted him, his hand on my shoulder and his words, face to face. He had his reasons. I had to know what those reasons were. He owed that to me. He had to tell me who had spoken to me in front of the black lake. Who was the man I had stood beside? A traitor cannot look upon his land that way. He cannot love his land like that. I drank.

At eleven o'clock, I returned to my workshop. I closed the iron shutter. I sat down. I was still trembling with cold. I hardly recognized myself. I took off my Irish ring. I threw it onto my workbench, to lose it. I buried Tyrone's cap among the blocks of wood. I struggled for breath. Tyrone's laugh. The redhead's limp. Jim's coffin crushing my shoulder. Tyrone's expression. His hood over his eyes. The crowd cheering him when he got out of prison. I tore down a photo of my traitor, pinned to the wall, in which we stood side by side. I pushed a violin out of the way and I slept, my head in my arms, searching for the anger of Mise Éire, my old woman, and crying for the love of my friend.

Interrogation of Tyrone Meehan by the IRA

18 DECEMBER 2006

—You don't have anything to say about the Frenchman?

—Tony? The violin-maker?

—Do you know any other Frenchman, Meehan?

—I know his parents, a few of his friends.

—It's him we're interested in.

—I don't see why.

—You're very close.

(Silence)

—Did you have any contact with the Brits in Paris?

—I've already said.

—Is that where they debriefed you?

(Silence)

—Was he involved in any of this?

—Tony?

—Yes, Meehan, Tony the Frenchman. Did he know you were betraying us?

—No.

—You went to Paris eight times. You stayed at his place, we know that. And you're trying to tell us that he didn't know?

—He didn't know.

—We will interrogate him.

—Leave him out of this.

—Then answer, Meehan.

—I have answered, Mike. He thought I was coming for the Movement. He didn't ask any questions.

—Did you tell him officially that you were there for the IRA?

—I didn't say anything. I think that's what he believed.

—You think?

—He was afraid for me.

—Do you know that he did some favours for us?

—Yes.

—You warned him against that. Why?

—It wasn't his war.

—How do you explain the fact that five volunteers who were operating in France were arrested in 1982?

(Silence)

—Answer, Meehan.

—I can't explain it.

—Did the Frenchman have anything to do with these arrests?

—He had nothing to do with them.

—And what about you, Meehan?

—No.

—Do you remember John McAnulty, the taxi driver from Ardoyne who had that big white beard?

—Yes.

—Do you know he thought he was grassed up?

—I know.

—The Frenchman didn't know that it was you who was grassing on them?

—It wasn't me.

—Did your employers know that you stayed with the Frenchman?

—Yes.

—Did you tell them?

—They knew.

—Did they also know that he had done favours for the IRA?

—I never said anything about the IRA.

—You have been lying for four days, Meehan.

—I am not lying.

—Did you, at any time, talk to the Frenchman about your betrayal?

—Never.

—Did you never feel like confiding in him?

(Silence)

—If he really knew nothing, it must have come as some fucking surprise to him, mustn't it?

—He didn't know anything.

—How do you think he took it?

—I don't know.

—You ratted on him too, Meehan. You ratted on five volunteers and one good lad who thought he was doing the right thing.

—I never ratted on anyone.

—Do you want us to put you face to face with the Frenchman?

—Leave him alone.

—Would you not like to know what he thinks of his Irish friend?

(Silence)

—Do you not give a fuck?

(Silence)

—Do you not give a fuck? Say it, Meehan. Say that you don't give a fuck about the Frenchman. You don't give a fuck about anything when you're a tout.

—*I don't give a fuck.*
—*Say it again for us, Meehan.*
—*I don't give a fuck.*
—*I don't give a fuck about the Frenchman. Say it.*
—*I don't give a fuck about the Frenchman.*

THE SECRET

I waited until Christmas to return to Belfast. Before that, I couldn't. The IRA released Tyrone on 21 December 2006. He left Dublin, alone. His family had heard nothing. Sheila and Jack were waiting for a sign from him. I called. Jack told me that I was welcome there. That I could come for Christmas, that we would go to Mass together and that we would share Christmas dinner. I arrived on Christmas Eve, at night. Nobody came to get me at the airport. It was even colder here than how I felt inside. I took the bus to the Europa Hotel, then a black taxi from Castle Street. I was in the back, squashed between a woman laden down with presents and a young man. Two men were facing me on the pull-down seats. In the front, a passenger was talking to the driver. I closed my eyes. I have always loved this moment when I come back. The group taxi. This entrance into Belfast, tightly surrounded by people. I have always loved these women who furtively bless themselves when they go past a cross, these solemn men, these children in wrinkled uniforms.

This time, I don't know. Everything was different. Sitting on their pull-down seats, the men were impenetrable. The woman pushed me out of the way as she got out. The glass panel that separates the driver was open. He had turned up the radio. It was explaining that Tyrone Meehan had maybe run off to England. That even his wife knew nothing. I looked at our street. The orange light from the lamp posts, pieces of paper in the wind. Since the IRA ceasefire, everything had calmed down. It was all hard to fathom. Not one military patrol, no jeeps. The police Land Rovers had shiny new coats of paint. Here, there, on the Glen Road or in Springfield, a British barracks was missing from the street; deserted, then demolished, transformed into a traffic island. And yet the British flag was still flying over the City Hall, the Unionists were still refusing to power-share, Protestant stones were still breaking the windows of isolated Catholic houses, a long wall was splitting Belfast in two; wariness was intact. Calm reigned like a misunderstanding. A British army Saracen drove past us, headlights on. A loudspeaker attached to the roof was playing a U2 song. In the turret, two girls in white shirts and English helmets were waving bottles of cider and singing. I had heard about this. It was now possible to rent out redundant military hardware for birthday parties, to visit the city, put it behind you, or to shock a violin-maker from Paris.

Sheila opened the door. She asked where my bag was. I did not have one. Just a change of clothes in a satchel. I had come with nothing. Jack recognized my voice. He came to the door; his step was heavy. He put his hand on the back of my neck and we embraced. On the doorstep, Sheila, Jack and me, without a word, our hands on each other's shoulders. In the living room there were two women I knew. They got up. I said, 'Tony from Paris.' 'A friend of Tyrone's,' added Sheila. I sat down on a chair. I didn't know where to look. Sheila brought me a cup of tea. It was scalding.

The women left. Last year I had put up a paper tree in the corner, beside the wooden crib. This year there was nothing. No decorations, no lights. Not even a Christmas card on the fireplace.

Sheila had made a lamb stew. One day, a long time ago, she told me that I should never count how many potatoes I was piling onto my plate. That since the Great Famine, counting them brought bad luck. That you had to eat them, and more again without thinking of tomorrow. I had brought a bottle of Beaujolais Nouveau. I filled my glass. Sheila was drinking tea. Jack had brought beer for himself. We said nothing. There were just those looks that speak volumes. I said the stew was good. Sheila thanked me. On the dresser in the living room was their wedding photo, him and her smiling.

—Tyrone is well, murmured Sheila.

She said it with her back turned, while she was bringing the stew dish back into the kitchen. We had hardly touched it. I wanted to talk. Jack took two cigarettes out of his packet and held one out to me. I don't smoke. He knows this. It was out of politeness. I looked at Sheila's frail shoulders. Her apron tied at the back, her short white hair. She bustled about doing nothing.

—Have you seen him? I asked.

She ran some water into the sink. Jack sat down in his father's armchair to put his shoes back on.

—I have seen him. He's fine, Sheila replied.

—Are you going to see him again?

—I am going to see him again.

There. That was it. I helped to clear the coffee table. Sheila was tired. Jack was going out again. Like many ex-Republican volunteers, he had become a doorman for the local pub. He would be home late. Since his release from prison, I had been sleeping in the living room. He asked me if I wanted his bedroom. I declined. He opened up the sofa bed and handed me a sheet and a blanket. He said he was happy that I was there. That we would have time to talk tomorrow. Then he hugged me and thanked me for coming.

∾

—Can you keep a secret? Tyrone Meehan asked me one day.

It was the end of summer, 1983. A few days earlier the IRA had caused carnage. A rural unit was to plant a bomb in a hotel in the middle of the countryside. Three volunteers had placed explosives on the outside window sills and two others were waiting half a mile away on the outskirts of the village, to give warning to the police and to a charity. That was the way they operated then. Twice, in Belfast, the British authorities had been slow to pass on the illegal organization's warning. People had been killed. Since then, the IRA had warned a neutral body, the Order of Saint Andrew, or the Good Samaritans, who could testify as to the time of the warning. The explosives had been primed to go off after forty-five minutes. Enough time for the security forces to evacuate the area. One minute after planting the bomb, an IRA volunteer went into the phone booth. The twisted wire was hanging down, the receiver pulled off. The telephone had been vandalized during the night. The two Republicans got into the car. They headed to the village in search of a pub and a public phone. The first phone they found was occupied. A woman laughing. In the second pub, the phone was sitting on the bar. It was from the third pub that they made the call, standing in the middle of the room and the snooker players. There were only seven minutes left. The police and the soldiers arrived as the bomb exploded. It was a unionist area but some old Catholic women had come specially to the hotel for a cat competition. There were twenty-four victims. Nine women and fifteen cats. The next day, a charred body had been drawn on a poster with the word 'murderers' written in black letters. Through the official channel, signed 'P. O'Neill, Dublin', the IRA had explained itself. Then offered an apology to the victims' families. In the press, on the radio, on the television, everywhere, the same words and the same images appeared. The IRA had killed ordinary people. The IRA was going after the elderly, cats, any living being. I found this unfair and revolting. I had been deeply affected by the news and disgusted by the posters. If that telephone booth had been working, only the hotel would have been blown up. There would have been no victims. And that would have been it. It would have made three lines in the *Belfast Telegraph* and not a word about it in the Parisian press. No worse than the blowing up of the Europa Hotel or the department stores in the city centre. The economic war, like everywhere else in Northern Ireland, and that was all.

—The IRA apologized. It explained. What more could it do?

—Maybe not plant these bombs, he replied.

I said they couldn't help it. That if the telephone booth had not been out of order, there would have been no victims.

—Without the bomb there would have been none either, replied my traitor.

So I began to talk about the clean war. I don't know why. I always had this word at the tip of my tongue when referring to the struggle led by the Irish Republicans. Clean war. A clean war. A war not in the name of religion like the anti-papists of the other side, not in the name of domination, like those on the other side, but in the name of freedom, democracy and equality. A war in which the enemy is the soldier, not the civilian. A war in which enough time is left to ensure there will be no victims before an attack on a public place. Yes, a war in which victims are a source of concern. Tyrone was looking at me. I remember that look. He was smoking, his cap on his head. He was in a corner of the room. Sheila had gone out.

There was him, me, and Jack in his golden frame. Tyrone spoke. He talked about the bomb attacks in Birmingham, Manchester, all those bombs planted with no warning in the middle of English crowds. I said that that was in the past, that it was a long time ago, that the IRA had changed, that it was waging a clean war. I, Antoine, Tony, the Parisian violin-maker, was explaining to Tyrone Meehan what war was being waged under his orders in his own country.

—Can you keep a secret? Tyrone Meehan then asked me.

He put out his cigarette and looked me straight in the eye. He looked different, now, from that day in front of the black lake, just before buying my cap. He told me that there was no such thing as a clean war. That I knew nothing about the war. Nothing. He told me that the IRA killed because it had to. That it would continue to do so for as long as it took. He asked me what I knew about IRA orders. About its strategy.

He told me that if sixteen Catholic children were killed tomorrow by British troops in the ghetto of Ardoyne, why wouldn't there be a retaliatory bomb in a school in London? Well? Why not? And without warning, on purpose, so as to have a maximum number of victims. What did I know about any of that? He asked me if I knew that he, Tyrone Meehan, was ready to carry out this act of death if he was given the order to do so. Did I know that he would do it, himself, reciting the names of the sixteen dead children? Did I have any doubts about this violence? Then no. Please, he said. The war is dirty. Dirty. Don't ever talk about clean war. Don't ever talk about it, not here, not anywhere, because tomorrow perhaps, we will make a liar of you. I looked at Tyrone. He lit a cigarette and winked at me. His friendly face. And then he turned towards the window and watched the rain. He had been betraying his own for two years.

Jack came home in the middle of the night, after his shift at the door of the pub. He bumped into the coffee table, swearing. He was drunk. I heard the armchair creaking. He sat down, his elbows on his knees and his head in his hands.

—Are you asleep, Tony?

I didn't answer. I watched him beneath lowered eyelids. He had kept his jacket on. His black tie had been loosened. His white shirt hung out over his trousers.

—I know you're not asleep.

He rubbed his cheeks roughly. He lit up a cigarette. He coughed a little. Sang a few notes from a Piaf song.

—No, rwien dé rwien ...

He asked me what the name of that French singer was. He stubbed out his cigarette. He knew I was listening. He threw his head back. He told me he had a shitty job, a shitty life, a shitty father. Said that the ceasefire had led to nothing. He was still as poor, still as Catholic and still as alone. He said that his mother cried morning, noon and night. That for three days the milkman had forgotten their door. That people looked at him like you would look at a rat. His only friends were those from prison. Three lads he'd introduce me to one day. He told me that when he'd got out he hadn't recognized anyone. He said that the prisoners had been forgotten. Since the peace process, the Republican party had been avoiding ex-prisoners. He and his prison comrades were not educated enough, not good enough, too unsophisticated, too rough-and-ready, had too many tattooes for the new world.

He recited names I did not know. Sinn Féin counsellors from the north and the south of Ireland, young lads with no past, girls who had never suffered, people who look good on posters, reassuring for everyone, who appeared out of nowhere, who know how to hold a conversation, not a gun. He told me he was angry. He felt betrayed. Not by his traitor of a father, but by the way life goes on. Everything was moving too fast. He had lost his his bearings. War was simple, black and white, a cemented suffering. Peace was too high a price to pay for the poor. Yesterday he was an IRA lieutenant and today he was just one more underemployed person. He said that there was no longer anything socialist about all this. That James Connolly, my handsome man with the round-collared shirt, had been had too. He talked and talked.

He told me that that morning, in Ballymena, a Catholic schoolboy on his way back after buying a pizza had been lynched to death in the middle of the street by Protestant kids his own age. He said that the unionists and Loyalists would never, ever want to share power with Catholics. That peace and the peace process should not be confused. He said that there would never be peace without justice. He quoted the mural slogans. He sang a little more Piaf. He wearily rubbed his beard. He said he hadn't told me anything. That he was sorry. He said he had faith all the same. He asked me to sleep. He said he had had a drop to drink. That he was sad. That it was exhaustion, disappointment and anger. He told me I had to see Tyrone. I had to. Not to believe him, but to see him. He said that he didn't have a father any more, either. That he too had been killed by the British. Not with a bullet, but with money. He told me I would have to grieve for him. He hummed 'No, rigrette rwien'. He got up from the armchair, sighing heavily. He went upstairs, to the bedroom of his childhood. To my room, back when he was a soldier.

∼

I had decided to spend a week in Belfast. I stayed for eleven days in all. On 29 December 2006, I met the IRA. Not the IRA in parade uniform, not the volunteers jumping over walls to cheers, not those women and men who fire salutes over the coffins of the comrades, but the Irish Republican Army like I had never seen it before. I was walking down the Falls Road that Friday night. A van stopped.

—Get in, Tony, a man said to me.

He was neither threatening nor smiling. He was as he had to be. He opened the back door, that's all. There were two of them in front. He gave me dark glasses with cotton wool taped to the lenses. He asked me to put them up against my eyes. He explained that it was for my own safety. If we were intercepted, I only had to say that I had been kidnapped. We drove for a long time. When we arrived, the man took me by the arm. I crossed a street. There were children's shouts, women's voices. I imagined myself, masked, firmly led forward, walking through this Irish indifference. A door opened. I felt the heat and smelt the tea. My glasses were removed. A woman with grey hair was standing there, offering me an egg and onion sandwich.

—Upstairs, said the man from the van.

I held my bread and a scalding mug. We went in to a narrow bedroom. Bed, crucifix, chair. The man sat down on the chair. He gestured towards the bed. He looked at me. He put his hands on his thighs. He was tall, with a hard face, short hair and a grey moustache. He looked embarrassed.

—Do you know who we are?

—I know.

That's how I answered. Like in a film where words are scarce. I was afraid, and yet I wasn't. I had nothing to fear from them. Nothing to fear from my friend in the round-collared shirt, nothing from my Jim, nothing from Jack who talked to me in the middle of the night while I slept. I had nothing to fear from the terrible beauty, nothing. The man told me that Tyrone had been interrogated by the IRA. That Tyrone had refused to collaborate with the Republican Army. And that he had exonerated me. The British agent had refused to answer all the questions he was asked. He told me that Tyrone might ask to see me. Me, the Frenchman, the violin-maker, the insignificant friend. He said that I was not to accept this invitation. He told me that Tyrone was in the Republic of Ireland, near the border. And that he was not safe. He told me that the Brits and Loyalists could try and get rid of him. If that happened the IRA would be suspected and the peace process jeopardized. He said that Tyrone Meehan had been a terrific man, a courageous Republican, a fearless volunteer. But now all that was in the past. The IRA would not touch Tyrone, because Tyrone no longer existed.

—He is like a dead man. He *is* dead. He died in November 1981, the first day he informed.

—You need to put it behind you and do your grieving, he said, before handing me a cigarette.

I replied that I hadn't understood everything. His accent, the way he finished each word with a Dublin 'sh'. He leaned over. He took my cigarette and slipped it back into the packet. He explained that if I visited Tyrone, I would be suspected of conspiring with a traitor. Or suspected of complicity with his enemies if anything happened to him. In both cases, my visit would be ill-advised. He told me that if I went ahead and saw him anyway, if Tyrone Meehan spoke, if he admitted things that he hadn't dared to tell the army he had betrayed, I would never be able to step foot in Ireland again. Never. Because I would be the holder of secrets that were much too big for me. If he confessed, if he admitted who his victims were, lots of people would want to hear me, one way or another, now, here and elsewhere and forever. Loyalists, dissident Republicans, all those who were opposed to the ceasefire, nationalist families who had been wondering all these years who had betrayed their son, who had sold their daughter, who had placed the British SAS ambush at the back of a Republican unit so that all eight of them were decimated one May night in 1987. They would want to know everything. I would have an answer to their suffering, but I would be able to reveal nothing. I would never be able to betray Tyrone Meehan. He would have spoken to me in secret, in confidence, as a brother. He would have sworn me to secrecy. And even if I talked, my lips would not be his. My words would not be his. No one would really hear me but everyone would hate me for having heard him. We would have a secret, he and I, that's all. A shared violence, a common betrayal, a responsibility, a complicity. And soon, there would be two exiled brothers.

THE SILENCE

Sheila drove slowly. We had passed over the border in Strabane and were heading towards Donegal. What border, at that? During the war, the secondary roads had been blocked by the British army. The soldiers would come at night, with lorries and bulldozers, and dump enormous blocks of stone on the road. In the morning, the residents of the villages would attempt to clear the way. Confrontations occurred everywhere. For the British, it was more effective militarily to control the main roads and to close off the dozens of back roads. Their observation towers, their helicopters, their patrols, their armoured jeeps made border movement by the IRA difficult. Since the peace process, all of that has disappeared. The observation towers have practically all been dismantled. The are no more patrols. There are no longer any boulders on country roads, no more police checkpoints, no more 'border', nothing. You just notice all of a sudden that number plates have changed and that kilometres have replaced miles on signposts.

It was Tuesday 2 January 2007. There was an icy wind. It had snowed during the night, but in the morning, all the white had disappeared. Sheila had told me that we would be leaving early. Jack was in Dublin. I slept in his room. I was awakened by a gentle knock on my door. The tea and toast were ready. Sheila did not talk. She would do as her husband wished, that was all. But she did not agree.

—It's crazy, she had sighed, when Tyrone asked to see me.

He had got a message out through Father Byrne, an old priest who had known Tyrone since he was a child. A short, simple sentence, which he had repeated word for word to Sheila.

—If the Frenchman wants to come, he's welcome.

Byrne wanted to see me. We met that same day in Divis Street, at St Peter's cathedral. He asked me if I was a Catholic.

—A wee bit, I answered.

He laughed. He said that around here, being a wee bit Catholic was already a lot. He brought me over to the front row of the choir. He knelt down. I followed his example. He told me that we were going to pray for Tyrone Meehan. He closed his eyes and bowed his head. We were almost alone. There were only a few old woman, who all appeared to be sleeping.

—If you want to see Tyrone, you're welcome to, the priest said.

I looked at him. He was still praying. He had whispered this between two holy words. His voice was strange, at once metallic and deep. The voice of a man who has no regrets.

Tyrone Meehan knew I was in Belfast. Sheila had seen him after his interrogation by the IRA. He had asked after her, after Jack. He also wanted to know how I was. When Sheila explained what was being said on the street, Tyrone silenced her by putting a finger on her lips. Sheila told me this in the car, while we were driving. She spoke in a tired voice. She answered my questions looking straight at the road. I asked her what Tyrone wanted to know about me. What I thought of his betrayal? What I said about it to others? Sheila shook her head. No. He wanted to know if I was all right. How I had been getting on these past five months. I hadn't seen him since 10 July 2006. We had said goodbye in summer and here we were, he and I, in winter.

~

—Would you like to see the Kesh? he had suggested last July.

The camp where Bobby Sands and his comrades died was going to be demolished. A commission had decided that the prison would be levelled and replaced by a stadium, a hotel complex, a multiplex cinema and shops. Republicans had fought to preserve the memory of the site. They had been unsuccessful. The British authorities refused the shrine but accepted the idea that some trace should remain, like the hospital in which the hunger strikers died. While they awaited the arrival of the first excavators, every day ex-prisoners, their families and their friends, came back to the camp. They wanted to see again, show again, tell again. The Republican movement made up the lists of visitors. The penitentiary administration organized the visit.

I had never been to Long Kesh. Just once, I had accompanied Sheila on a visit to see Jack, but stayed in the car, in the car park. I accepted Tyrone's invitation. There were nine of us in a minibus. My traitor, three ex-prisoners, their wives, a child and me. The representative from the Northern Ireland Office smiled as she came to meet us. She asked if there were any ex-residents among us. The men lifted their hands. She wished them welcome. Then we walked. Amidst the silence, the barbed-wire enclosures, the heavy doors, the high walls, the gates, the redundant watch towers, the torn corrugated iron and the wild weeds. We walked for an hour. The clouds were heavy with rain. In the corridors, in the deserted cells, the men were silent. There were still blankets on the beds, fallen curtains, round aluminum ashtrays. There were slop buckets on the wardrobes, faded paper towels on the shelves. Coming out of H-Block 4, the ex-prisoners were reunited with their little exercise yard. A square courtyard, a wire fence all around, with a basketball net and the remains of painted goalposts on the ground. While they smoked a cigarette, Tyrone and the three others took up their old positions. Backs against the fence, legs bent, a captive look about them. One of them sat down on a step, in the corner that was his, passing his finger again and again over a groove in the stone that he had furrowed. Another crouched down under an awning, the back of his neck pressed against a ledge. He smiled at me. He told me he had spent eighteen years in this here place, sitting on his heels and looking up to the sky. He spoke breathlessly. He coughed a lot. He was elegant and delicate. He had been on hunger strike when the 1981 movement had ended. The depravation and suffering had been with him ever since.

I followed Tyrone. He said nothing to me, did not look at me. I felt superfluous. He looked at the barbed sky. He ran his fingers lightly over a cell door. He placed his palm on a stained mattress. Like the others, this was the first time he had been back here. I did not leave his side. He seemed infinitely sad and old. When we went into the hospital, he put his hand on his chest.

—Bobby Sands' cell is number 8, murmured the civil servant who was accompanying us.

And then she went out to leave us alone.

I went in first. The room was tiny, the walls dirty, the paint sickly. In front of the window, there was an iron bed base, narrow and tired. Here it was. Right here. I sat down on the bed. I listened to the steps of the others in the corridor. I closed my eyes, my hands flat on the icy springs. I saw Bobby Sands' face again. His never-ending smile. I felt a pain in my stomach, a rod cutting into my chest, a violent headache. I think I stopped breathing.

Tyrone Meehan came in. I got up. He took off his cap and stood with his back to the wall. Then he looked at me. I was shaking. He asked me to leave him alone. He asked me with his head down and an inscrutable expression on his face. I was surprised. I went out of the cell, out of the hospital. I had tears in my eyes. I waited outside. It was raining. The right kind of weather. I was breathing fast. My head was spinning. I felt weak, lonely, far from everything. I thought of my Parisian street corner, my workshop, the smell of varnish, of my midday sandwich with pickles. I think I was afraid.

Tyrone Meehan had been crying. He came back out, his cap on his head and his hands in his pockets. His cheeks were red, his mouth open, a trail of snot carelessly wiped across his cheek. He drew the sleeve of his jacket across his mouth and came towards me.

—Listen carefully to what I'm going to say to you, wee Frenchie, whispered my traitor.

He stood up straight. He hadn't yet recovered his normal expression, his smile. He was bloodless. Pale and grey. His mouth was dry. The corners of his lips were stuck together.

—Listen, and don't say anything.

There he was, in front of the door of the hospital, in the middle of the fenced-in enclosure. There he was, so worried. He put his hands on my shoulders and looked at me.

—I love you, son.

—Me too, I smiled.

Tyrone Meehan closed his eyes. He shook his head.

—Don't say anything. Please, listen.

He looked at me again. His expression was serious and his hands heavy.

—I love you, my traitor said once again.

~

Sheila looked tired. She switched on the radio. It was a programme in Irish. I leant my forehead against the freezing window. For a long time, we drove along a black lake. I saw our lake again, with our tent and Tyrone telling me not to be afraid. I wondered if he sometimes went to England. Or to Scotland. If there was another lake over there, and another violin-maker whom he hugged and smiled at. I wondered why no one had ever noticed anything about his betrayal. Neither his wife, nor his son, nor his comrades-in-arms, nor I. How did he do it? How had he done it? How was he doing it today? And what if he had made a complete double life for himself? Another life just for him? I imagined him going into another house, in Scotland, let's say. A big house, a loopy dog against his legs, hanging up his soft cap and his tweed jacket in a secret wardrobe until he took the boat back to Ireland and become himself again. I imagined him whistling as he changed, looking in a full-length mirror, putting on pleated, green woollen trousers turned up at the bottom, straightening a white linen shirt and buttoning up a grey mohair cardigan. I imagined him coming down a big staircase to be with Molly, his wife and Charles, his slightly goofy grown-up son. I imagined him hunting, wearing a blue-green tartan cap with red threaded through it, and a worn Barbour jacket. I imagined him talking about us, about me, or saying nothing, forgetting all that as he contemplated the blackness of a loch.

I imagined him in Paris, coming out of my bedsit. And then what? Where did he go then? Who did he see? I imagined him in a restaurant with two English people, a man and a beautiful woman whom he made laugh. His back was to the street so that he would not be seen. I imagined him drinking wine and eating fish. Why fish? Because he didn't like it. So this meant that with them he had to order sea bream and be delighted that it was pink at the bone. He had to smoke something other than his Gallagher. I imagined him lighting up a Dunhill and putting on airs. What did he say to the English? Did he give names? Did he tell them about secret meetings? Did he give them the position of an arms cache? I would never know. All I could hear was the woman laughing. That's it. I have it. I know. He would make fun of the Irish. He would ridicule their struggle and their suffering. That was why the woman was laughing. It was not a work lunch. It was a lunch with friends, beside the British embassy, with anti-Irish jokes at the end of the meal. I imagined him getting up first, shaking the man's hand and kissing the woman. He kissed her. She gave him an envelope. When he kissed her, she slipped an envelope into his jacket pocket. Actually no, not an envelope. An envelope was impossible. That's just in old films. Franz Lang scenarios. No. He just kissed her the way you say goodbye to a colleague. His English colleague. His smiling colleague who works in the enemy embassy.

—We're here, Sheila said.

I was asleep, with my mouth open. I caught a trail of dribble with a flick of my tongue. My back ached. At a crossroads, in the middle of the countryside, there were two Garda cars. And another one, with no recognizable sign, a little farther away, three men inside and a fourth leaning against the hood. Sheila slowed down. She passed by the police vehicle. The guard bent down, recognized her. He nodded to her and made a note of something in his notebook.

Tyrone Meehan had told me about his father's house. I had never come here. It was a farm, a whitewashed bungalow with a thatched roof, at the edge of a forest. A light trail of smoke rose from the chimney. We parked on the wayside. Sheila hit the horn three times with her fist. We waited. And then the door opened. Tyrone Meehan appeared. He had an Aran cardigan under his tweed jacket. He was wearing his soft cap and a scarf tied around his neck. He came out onto the doorstep. He looked right and left. He locked the door and gestured at me to follow him into the forest.

—I'll come back and get you in an hour, Sheila said.

I asked her if she wanted to stay. She shook her head. Sheila Meehan had never been a great talker. On nights out, in the pub, among friends, she was always subdued. Since the betrayal, she had walled herself in.

I walked towards him through the wind, past the dead trees. He broke a branch off an ash to make a walking stick for himself. He had tucked his trousers into his boots. No noise. Just his footsteps, and mine, on the winter frost.

—We'll get some wood for the fire, Tyrone said.

He bent down. I did the same. For several minutes, without a word, we collected the damp, cold wood.

—Is that enough? I asked, showing him what I had.

—There's never enough, replied Tyrone.

And then he bent down again, kicking over a log. When he raised his head, his eyes met mine. I had not yet looked him in the eye. For eighteen days I had been waiting for this moment. I had thought about it every night. It had kept me awake. What would be the look on Tyrone Meehan's face? Would he have lost his sparkle? Are your eyes darker when you have betrayed? Different? Are they covered by a veil? A dull black silk veil? Can you recognize a traitor by looking him in the eye? Tyrone lifted his head and our eyes met. We stayed like that for a few infinite seconds. Me bending down, he half-standing. It was Tyrone Meehan. A little more alone, perhaps, a little worried too, but he still had a smile in the corner of his eyes and his deep wrinkles etched right over to his temples. And then he stood up. I did the same. We went into the house.

There was a big room with empty walls and a clay floor. There was a door: a bedroom, probably. A sink without water. There was a gas lamp on the table and candles everywhere. My traitor went over to the fire. He set down his bundle of wood. I set mine down in the corner. He knelt down, puffing. It looked like his back was hurting him, his knees too. He scrunched up some paper, set a few sticks on top of it and sprayed the pile with petrol from a lighter. The flame was instant and bright. He got up again and threw a few logs onto the fire. Then he stayed like that, facing the hearth, his hands in his pockets, his back to me.

—You can sit down, said my traitor.

I pulled out a chair and sat at the table. It was all so quiet; the only sound came from the crackling hearth. Tyrone took off his cap, hit it against his thigh and put it in the back pocket of his trousers. I was cold. The same cold I had felt in my workshop when I heard about his treachery. My throat was tight. I could see my breath.

—What do you want to know, Tony? asked my traitor.

I leant forward and placed my hands between my thighs. This, too, I had thought about, cried over so many times; walking in Paris, shaking in my workshop, lying down, feverish, falling like I had died, on the bed in the hideout. I had told myself that when I faced him I would look at him. He would have his head down and his hands would be wearily by his side. And I would ask him. Why? First of all. Why did you do this, Tyrone Meehan? Why do people do this, Tyrone Meehan? What breaks inside us? Tell me, Tyrone Meehan. Where does this poison come from? From the head? From the heart? From your stomach? Is it a battle or a surrender? What is it like to betray, Tyrone Meehan? Does it hurt? Does it make you feel good? Could it happen to anyone? To me, just like it happened to you, Tyrone?

I remember this asshole, a right bastard, a piece of scum, droning on at the head of the table at the end of a Parisian meal. He had had a lot to drink. I can't remember what our conversation was about. He claimed he would never speak under torture. Never. He said he knew, he felt it deep down, that he was of that race of men. His wife put her hand on his. She smiled at him. She was proud. I had had too much to drink, too. I took a knife, got up and suggested we give it a try. He said I was crazy. I screamed. I threw the knife onto the ground and I left. Is that it, Tyrone? Is it like that? You think you're going to hold out, you say you will, you live with that certainty and then something happens to your soul that is stronger than anything? Then what? How can you bear the touch of others, when you are a traitor? A traitor to your wife, your son, your friends, your comrades, to the old women that cheered you in the rain when you honoured the Republic. How can you kiss the cheek of those you have betrayed? What is it like, Tyrone Meehan, to hold a man's shoulder in front of a black lake, to shake the hand you are deceiving, to sell friendship, love, hope and respect? What is it like, Tyrone, to find yourself face to face with your Parisian violin-maker?

—What do you want to know? I'm listening, son.

—Nothing, I said.

I said 'Nothing' and I bowed my head. I looked at the door. I regretted all this time Sheila had given me. The fire was battling with the damp. The smoke came out heavy and white. Again, Tyrone stoked it. Then he went over to the dresser. He took out two beakers. He heated some water on the one-ring stove.

—Milk?

—No thanks.

He wasn't looking at me. He walked heavily around the room. He was all right. He was doing what he had to without a thought for me. He sat down. He and I, face to face with our two scalding beakers. I closed my hands over the metal. He brought the tea to his lips. He looked at me. He said:

—Do you want to know if any men died because of me?

—No!

I shouted. I raised a hand so suddenly that I spilt my tea all over the table. I stretched my hand out, fingers spread. I raised it in front of him to keep him quiet.

—Do you not want to know?

I didn't answer. I drank what was left of my tea. He got up to get a sponge and some lemon biscuits.

—Do you not want to know?

—I don't know.

—You don't know?

I didn't know. I knew nothing any more. I was wondering why I had come here.

—Why did you come here?

—I don't know.

—You don't know.

Tyrone Meehan sighed. I shrugged my shoulders. Nothing was happening as I had imagined it. It was he who was talking, he who was asking the questions and I who was remaining silent. I was the one who was embarrassed. I was the one who felt guilty and dirty.

—You know you can never come back to Ireland?

The IRA had already told me. I looked at my traitor. I was neither sad nor worried; I felt nothing. That's just the way it was.

—I know.

How could I tell him that I didn't care? That *he* was Ireland. Jim and he were the only Ireland I had ever known. How could I tell him that I already no longer had my place here? I looked around the dark room, closed off from daylight. I looked at the table, our beakers, our hands. I shivered. Perhaps my Ireland was here. In this promise of darkness, these walls tired from the damp, this crude earthy floor, this sparse furniture, these candles, this bucket for the well. My Ireland had followed my traitor. He had captured it, taken it with him into exile.

—And what about our friendship?

My question came from my throat. It had been there since day one. Is a traitor a traitor all the time? Night? Day? When he is eating? When he laughs? When he winks in that old friendly way? Are you a traitor when you breathe? When you watch the sunset? When you go through the door of a church? When you greet someone in the street? When you say, looking at the sky, that it is going to rain? Are you a traitor when you pull up the collar of your jacket to keep out the cold? When you teach a Frenchman how to take a piss?

—What about our friendship?

—Was it real?

—I don't understand your question.

Tyrone got up again to feed the fire. He had his back to me. He turned around with the poker in his hand.

—Are you asking me if I am your friend?

I nodded. He came back to the table.

—That's why you came this whole way, wee Frenchie?

I whispered yes.

—And what do you think?

I looked at him. I did not like his smile. Or his eyes. He was sitting there, calm, his arms crossed on the table. It was up to me to explain myself. He got up, took his cap out of his pocket and put it back on his head.

—Look at me and tell me what you think.

—I don't know.

—You don't know much, do you?

I looked up at him. His eyes were blazing.

—I don't owe you anything, wee Frenchie. I don't owe anybody anything. I fucked up, son. I did what I did and that is my business.

My traitor got up. He went to the window. He lifted the curtain. He could probably see a corner of the forest and the bend in the road.

—I don't know if you have seen that film, *The Informer*, by John Ford?

I nodded. I stared at his back.

—Do you remember that guy, Gypo Nolan? He's the one who sells his friend Frankie McPhillip to the English? I've watched that film many times. I bought the tape in Dublin and I hid it in a cushion in the sofa. I used to watch it over and over when I was on my own. And you know what? For me, the most moving moment is Nolan's face in front of the poster, a shipping company offering a one-way to America for £10. Do you remember that part, wee Frenchie?

I said I did.

—Nolan was poverty-stricken and he drank. His only treasure was Katie, a Dublin prostitute, lonely and poor, like himself, who he dreamt of taking to America. Do you remember?

—Yes.

—And do you remember Nolan's eyes in front of the British Wanted poster? On it, there's McPhillip's face, his friend, and £20 in big print underneath. Exactly what's needed to get two people to America.

Tyrone Meehan came back over to the table. I started at the sound of a horn. Sheila had arrived.

—Do you know why I am telling you all this, son?

—No.

—Because I do not judge Gypo Nolan. I do not judge him because I am Gypo Nolan. You are Gypo Nolan, wee Frenchie. We all have a Gypo Nolan inside us. No one is born a complete bastard, wee Frenchie. The bastard is sometimes a great guy who just gives up. And now you are going to have to fight against Gypo Nolan, wee Frenchie. Against your one, the one you are hiding from us. Otherwise you're going to fuck up like me. You're going to end up like me. And you're going to die like me.

My traitor looked at me. He smiled at my surprise.

—Did no one tell you that I am going to die, son?

I said no with my eyes. Tyrone shrugged his shoulders.

—My God! You really don't know anything about this country.

Sheila beeped the horn once again. Tyrone Meehan got up. He went to the door. He waved wearily to her. I got up. My traitor turned around. He was just outside, I was still in. I wished he would take me by the shoulder, as he had done so many times. He stayed with his hands in his pockets. His smile had died with the open door.

—You haven't answered me, I murmured.

He looked at me and there was no sparkle any more. Then he moved out of the way to let me pass. He stayed on the stone doorstep; my feet were on the frozen ground. Then he opened his arms. The wool smelt of damp. We stayed like that, a second together. And then he gently pushed me away.

—I don't have an answer for you.

And then he turned around. He went back into his father's house, his house, no one's house. I saw his hunched back, his messy white hair, his soft cap. I saw his muddy boots, his creased trousers. I saw his hand wave goodbye. I never saw his eyes again, ever.

Interrogation of Tyrone Meehan by the IRA

20 DECEMBER 2006

—We're stopping, Tyrone.
 —Am I free to go?
 —That's right.
 —But I want to stay in Ireland.
 —We don't want to know.
 —Maybe not, but now you know.
 —So?
 —I am staying in Ireland and you know it. That's all.
 —It no longer concerns us.
 —But you know.
 —So what?
 —And it's not in your interests to let anything happen to me.
 —That's correct.
 —And so nothing is going to happen to me.
 —It is no longer our problem.
 —Don't mess me around, Mike O'Doyle.

—*I'm not messing you around, Tyrone.*

—*If the IRA doesn't want anything to happen to me, then nothing will happen to me.*

—*The IRA doesn't want anything.*

—*That sentence doesn't mean anything.*

—*What do you want, Meehan? Protection?*

(Silence)

—*You are on your own, Meehan. A scumbag of a man all on his own. With no community, no respect, nothing. For four days we have been questioning you for nothing. You didn't even talk to get it off your chest, so off you go. You are free, Meehan.*

—*You know right well where I'm going to live now.*

—*That does not interest us.*

—*I am going home, to Killybegs in Donegal.*

—*Shut the fuck up, Meehan.*

—*Now you know.*

—*We don't want to know anything.*

—*Home, to my father's house.*

—*Shut it, Meehan.*

—*You know everything. You know where I'm going to hide as soon as I have gone out that door. You can't do a thing against me any more.*

—*We're stopping here, Meehan.*

—*If anything happens to me, everyone will think it was you.*

—*I'm telling you again that you are free.*

—*Are your men going to kill me?*

—*You're free for fuck's sake. Get up now.*

—*Answer me, Mike, in the name of my dead father.*

—*Leave Pat Meehan out of this mess.*

—*I am not talking to you. I am talking to Mike O'Doyle.*

—*Let it go, Meehan.*

—*Mike, tell me nothing is going to happen to me.*

—Don't see anyone, don't talk to anyone and nothing will happen to you.

—Tell me that the IRA isn't going to do anything to me.

—It won't do anything, Meehan. Because you are nothing now.

—Can I go?

—We're asking you to go.

—Nothing will happen to me?

—Sort that out with the other crowd.

—What other crowd?

—There's not just the IRA, Meehan.

—Who are you talking about?

—You are a traitor. That means you have a lot of people against you.

—Is that a threat?

—That's enough. The interrogation stops here.

—Answer me! Is that a threat?

—We are stopping here, Meehan.

—What do I do now?

—You fend for yourself.

—You are responsible for what happens to me.

—Why? Who says so, Meehan?

—Everyone! Everyone will say that it was the IRA.

—Put your coat on.

—Mike! Say something for fuck's sake, Mike O'Doyle!

—Get up, Meehan. You're leaving.

—This is my death warrant. You know that, Mike.

—We're stopping everything, for God's sake. Cut that frigging camera.

GYPO NOLAN

With slow, heavy strides, Gypo emerges from a narrow, foggy brick lane strewn with greasy paper. He lights up a cigarette. He is wearing a huge, wide, flat cap, a jacket that is a little too small for him, a collarless shirt, a shabby waistcoat and has a scarf around his neck. It is dark. On the other side of the street, Katie lowers her shawl so that the short man can see her; she has undone the top button of her bodice. She is wearing a feather headdress. The man moves closer. He is a client. From another world than Katie's. Wearing a heavy coat, a bowler hat with a band around it, pale gloves, a wing collar, a pinned silk tie. He looks at her. He smiles meaningfully. He scrapes a match off the lamp post beside her, takes a drag from the cigarette and exhales the white smoke into the young woman's face.

Gypo comes upon the scene. He stops suddenly, arms outstretched, mouth open. He narrows his eyes, scowls, throws his cigarette over his shoulder, hurries over, picks the customer up with both hands and tosses him into the street.

—Gypo! scolds Katie Madden.

She shakes her head, looking up at her bullish man. He is like a child, his eyes sorrowful.

—What's the use, Gypo? I am hungry and I can't pay the room rent. Can you afford to pay for a room for me? Don't look at me like that, Gypo. You're all I have in the world. You're the only one I love and you know it. But how can we escape from this life?

She turns around. Behind her, in a shop window she sees a model boat and an advertisement offering boat passage to America for £10.

—Look, it's taunting us! she says pointing at the advert.

She comes over to Gypo. She murmurs to him.

—£10 for America. £20 and we would be free!

Why are you saying that? groans her man.

—What? £20?

—What are you getting at?

Gypo Nolan throws himself at her. He pushes her over.

—Go on then! Go and earn your £20 with that scum!

She stands back up. She juts out her chin.

—Saint Gypo! You think you're too good for me? You're no better than the rest of them! You're all the same! Keep your grand principles. I can't afford them!

She goes off. He lingers in the mist. He calls after her but to no avail.

Earlier on, he had come upon a poster pasted up on the walls of the city by the English, a Wanted for Murder sign. On it was the name of his friend, Frankie McPhillip, a member of the IRA on the run, and £20 in large, black letters. And he had wondered. He had wondered whether this money wouldn't put an end to their misery. And he wonders now if that's what Katie had been asking him. That's why he'd thrown himself at her and shaken her, out of sadness, anger and shame.

Katie has gone. She has left Gypo. He goes back up the street, hands in his pockets and his face sad. Again he passes by the shop with the model boat and the poster. He stands there in the dark, his face torn. This is the moment Tyrone spoke of, that precise instant. My traitor's favourite. The actor Victor McLaglen is a mere shadow in the street, his face barely lit by a nearby lamp post. He stares at the poster for a long time. His eyes are huge. His contorted face betrays his turmoil. He lowers his head, wipes his brow, his eyes, his mouth. He is crying. He glances up at the poster one last time. The light catches his expression. He is relieved. His choice is made. He will inform.

∼

Back home, I bought myself John Ford's *The Informer*.
—Is it a Western? asked the shop assistant.
—No, it's a film about the war in Ireland.
His question did not irritate me. I even smiled. I had a vague recollection of the story. The trembling clarity of Murnau's *Nosferatu*, expressions flooded with light, whimpered words, theatrical gestures, hands on hearts. I didn't buy it for Gypo Nolan, Katie Madden and Frankie McPhillip, but for Tyrone Meehan, to walk a while with him. I wanted to be there, with him, on his sofa, like all those times when he would wait for the French violin-maker to go home and for Sheila to fall asleep upstairs so he could slide the tape into the video recorder. 'Then Judas repented himself and cast down the thirty pieces of silver and departed.' Tyrone would read this sentence, which filled the whole screen, every time, even before the film began. I read it too. I sat on the floor, at home, alone, thinking of the house in Donegal, the candles, the fire in the hearth. I could see Tyrone in the forest, bent over a stump. I

watched the actor Victor McLaglen admitting to his IRA friends that he was the rat.

~

—I didn't know what I was doing, whimpers Gypo Nolan.

He is sitting on a bench, in a big room, surrounded by armed men wearing caps and trench-coats. He stands up, gripping Commander Gallagher's lapels with his two hands.

—I don't know! Do you understand what I'm saying to you?

He is lost for words. Breathless. He reaches out towards another volunteer, Bartley, who remains impassive. He turns around. He implores. He cries. He looks from face to face. His undone cravat is damp with sweat.

—Lads! Is there not one man here who can tell me why I did this?

Gypo Nolan falls heavily back down onto the bench, his face in his hands.

—My head hurts. I can't say why I did it. I don't know why.

~

The day after I saw Tyrone, I drank. I went to Jim's pubs. All of them, or near enough, for a single whiskey, standing at the bar, head back and eyes closed. I made my way up the Falls Road, ringing the bells of wire-screened doors. Each time, someone came over to me. I was the Frenchman, the violin-maker, the traitor's friend. There were no reproaches, no ill-feelings. I sensed something like compassion. They embraced me, looked into my eyes, shook my hand, bought me beers. They wondered why. Why him? Why Tyrone Meehan? One man said we should be looking for the woman.

The woman?

The woman, repeated the man, nodding his head.

—A mistress, do you mean?

I thought of Sheila. I had never seen Tyrone make eyes at any woman. I had never seen him make the slightest gesture or be suggestive in any way.

—You don't tout for twenty-five years because of a woman, said his wife.

—It depends on the woman, replied her husband.

He scowled. He said that you could imagine Meehan having an affair with the wife of an IRA officer in prison. A moment of weakness in peacetime, an act of betrayal in wartime. He spoke as though he knew what he was talking about. He turned to his wife. He told her that when he was behind bars himself, the idea that she might be unfaithful would have destroyed him.

—Now imagine that the Brits find out about it and have it on him, the man went on.

He looked at me solemnly, beer in hand.

—So what does he do, your Meehan? He keeps a low profile. He informs.

—Bollocks! Blackmail might work once, but not all these years, said an old man drinking at the bar.

He said he did not know Meehan, but he had seen plenty of informers in his time. For money, for pride, to end the violence, out of revenge after an IRA punishment beating, or after being sidelined from the Movement. He said he'd seen it all. And that he had even read a book written by an informer. Finishing up his beer, he explained that the Brits tried to seduce the traitor, not to force him. He said that a good traitor was a happy man, pampered, highly regarded by his new masters. That he needed to be appreciated and that's what he was made to feel. He said that a good traitor could not hate the other side. That he couldn't be held either by force or by blackmail. That blackmail and force made him volatile, versatile, weak and valueless for the enemy. He said that and then set down his beer. He turned to leave, shrugged and wondered aloud why he was telling me this.

Jack was the doorman at McDaid's. I had drunk a lot. He let me in all the same. Sitting on his stool, jerking his thumb towards the door, a man swore to me that Tyrone had done it to protect his son. Most likely. He thought that by collaborating with the enemy, his Jack would have his sentence shortened, that he would be released sooner. It has happened before, he insisted. You give them information, they free your wife or your kid. You refuse, they keep them in for as long as they need.

In the Busybee, a Republican told me that after Jim's funeral, Meehan was held responsible for what happened; they must have threatened him with a sentence of several years, maybe even life. They stick two or three murders on you and that's it. Life. It makes a soldier think and it can make a man think. He had just got out of prison. He didn't want to go back. That's why he gave in, the guy explained, lighting a cigarette.

In Kittie's, someone said he'd known a man like that. A gambler, a sick man, a man with a split personality, who informed for the rush, the risk, just like you'd jump off a bridge attached to an elastic cord. One woman reckoned that Tyrone was tired and that he wanted the war to end. Another wondered whether he was a double agent, whether the IRA hadn't ordered him to play the traitor to help the Republic. A young lad from Ardoyne shrugged, saying that you shouldn't try and understand traitors, but get rid of them.

Two others refused to speak to me. An elderly lady heard that Tyrone might have had an English grandfather. Another explained that her own son had won a holiday to Greece eight years ago. His name had been pulled out of a hat in a raffle. It was perfect timing. He was getting out of Long Kesh. He and his wife went to collect their prize in a big Belfast hotel. They ended up in a room with three men, one with a strong English accent. On the table were plane tickets and £3956 in cash in an open bag, exactly what they needed to pay off their car. The men introduced themselves as the British Force Research Unit. They knew everything about the couple. They told the woman that the money was theirs if they helped to stop the killings. If they agreed to give some information. She started shouting for help. Her husband kicked over a chair. They escaped from the hotel and went straight to the Sinn Féin press centre.

In the Rock Bar, too, people spoke of money. Tyrone was paid for information. He had admitted it at the press conference. No one knew how much, but it couldn't have been a lot. The IRA monitored suspicious movements in bank accounts. Tyrone Meehan had never attracted any attention. He was never seen dressed other than in his faded tweeds. In twenty-five years, he'd bought two second-hand cars. He drank normally and stood his round. He didn't gamble and he didn't do drugs. Sheila and he went to Paris once, and twice to Spain. They spent their holidays in a caravan park on the Antrim coast. What else could it be? There had to be something. And incidentally, where was he now? No one had seen him. In England, under a false name? Or in America? Or in Australia, with his face re-modelled? What did they all know? And what did I know? Did I want to know, really? Did I really and truly want to know?

—Do you know something, Frenchie?

Nothing. At all. My head was heavy. Drunkenness. I was barely listening. The sound of glasses, slurred voices. The rush for last orders before the bar shutter came down. I looked at these men; I saw Tyrone's back, as he busied himself rekindling the fire.

—What do you want to know, Tony?

Nothing, I answer. What an idiot! I don't want to know anything. I act the wise guy. I delude myself into thinking I'm above that. Nothing: it's your secret, Tyrone Meehan. I respect you, everyone and everything. Know, me? Don't you even think of it, Tyrone Meehan! I'm not the sort. Know what? Why you did this? Me, know that? Surely not! It doesn't matter. It's done. It could just as easily have happened to me. We all have a little Gypo Nolan up our arses, Tyrone Meehan. I came here because I wanted to know what you thought of me all these years. Of me, Tyrone Meehan. Was I really your friend? Will you tell me? You didn't betray me, did you? Seriously, Tyrone. Betray your wife, your son, your country, your honour, your freedom: yes, but don't tell me you betrayed me, too! Tyrone! You're not my traitor, are you? Tell me it's not true! Tell me, Tyrone Meehan!

In the Beehive, I went outside to throw up. A woman who knew him came to talk to me about Tyrone. She said there was no shame in having loved him, and to love him still. That didn't mean he was right; it didn't excuse anything. She said that Sheila loved him for what he was in the first place. A loving husband, elegant, attentive, funny, often weak, who looked out for her and their child. A traitor or a dead man, he was still the one she had shared her life with, laughing with him, singing with him, crying with him, fighting by his side day after day to protect their family from the flames of war. She told me that Jack loved Tyrone as a father. And that I had to accept my friendship with him. I wasn't really listening. I was faltering. I vomited again. In an alley behind the pub. Bent over, crouched down the way women do when pissing.

Red's was closing. It was almost midnight. At the door, the two men wouldn't let me in. I insulted them in French.

I drank one last beer in Burn's. The bar shutter was down. I took a half-finished Guinness from an empty table. People were putting their coats on. I had to close one eye to see better. I raised the glass. Half-full. I dragged a chair over. I sat down. The light was being switched on and off to tell us to leave. I looked around me. No Irish flag, no Republican posters. No national anthem to finish off the evening. Nothing. Is that what peace means, then? You just forget everything? Bobby? Connolly? All the others? You just put your coat on and go home?

~

In the film, Gypo Nolan the informer escapes. An IRA man finds him. He is wearing a soft hat, a belted trench-coat. He has a Lüger in his hand. His expression speaks of death. He fires four times.

GRÁINNE O'DOYLE

I knew. There was a pain in my chest and my shoulders when I got up. On 6 April 2007 my phone rang at about eleven o'clock. A voice I knew, metallic and deep. I hadn't seen Father Byrne since that time at St Peter's Cathedral. On the phone he called me Antoine. He liked that name. He had explained that St Anthony was the patron saint of prisoners and castaways and that Meehan was both of those at the same time.

—Tyrone is dead, Antoine.

I knew. I had always known. I feared for him from the first time our eyes met. I knew when I found out about his betrayal. He had told me. Everyone had told me. I put down the receiver. I felt nothing. It was Good Friday, nine years since the agreement that had led to the peace process. I hid my face in my hands. Not to cry, just for a little darkness. I tried to picture him. I tried the house in Donegal. His back to the fireplace, his voice, the steaming tea, his expression, the weight of his hands on my shoulder. But nothing.

Tyrone the traitor wasn't right for me. I needed something from before the lie. An image of my Tyrone intact.

Leaning on the workbench, I pressed my knuckles to my eyes. I was beside a platform, one arm around a wooden post. I was watching Tyrone, and a handful of Irish people. I looked from one to the other, smiling. I remember that it was raining. A spray coming in from the sea and whipping around the bay. Rain dripped from my cap. I smelt of dampness. It was 22 August 1998, in the main square in Killala, a coastal village in County Mayo. Hands on his hips, Tyrone Meehan was talking, without a mike, about 'The Year of the French'. He was reminding his audience that right here, 200 years ago to the day, and almost to the hour, General Humbert and a thousand or so French soldiers disembarked from three vessels that had come from La Rochelle to defend the Irish uprising. He spoke with his fist in the air, catching my eye between words. He told them about the battle. A handful of French at the head of an army of beggars come to welcome them. Soldiers of the land, peasants with nothing, no uniform, no weapons, a motely crowd bristling with lances, steel prongs fastened to quivering sticks. He was telling them about the blacksmiths and farriers, young and old, who had hammered these derisory spears together in every village. He told them about the English enemy, its red livery, its power, the strength of its weapons. He told them about our defeat. I watched him. I was smiling. He was wearing a sky-blue shirt that I had brought him from Paris.

—My fancy shirt, Tyrone used to say.

In the evenings, he would wash it with tar soap in the bathroom sink, letting it dry overnight so that he could wear it the next day. Sometimes it was still wet, like this morning, but he wore it anyway. Only a handful of people were there. A few elders; five or six children. Two of them were brandishing an Irish flag. A young girl had made a French flag, red, white, blue, which she had tied upside down to a stick. They all cheered when Tyrone finished speaking. People had come to hear him, and also to see him. He came from Belfast. His name was well known. He had done time. He appeared in photos beside important figures. He had known Bobby Sands in prison. He was serious and funny at the same time. When he got off the platform, he put his arm around my shoulder and called me 'General Tony'. He asked if he had been good, if people had listened. If I was proud of him. He refused an umbrella, saying the weather suited him fine. He adjusted his cap. I fixed mine too. We turned up our coat collars and walked towards the pub.

That night Tyrone made me talk about myself. About my father, my mother, my brother, my profession. He wanted to know what the Vosges and a French childhood had been like; he wanted to know the names of my wines, the names of my trees. He listened, leaning on the table with his head in his hands. He drank his beer with a smile. He looked straight at me, making me repeat words, laughing when he didn't understand. Here, in this tiny pub, in this insignificant village, men came and touched him on the shoulder, women held out their hands to him. People who had missed the ceremony apologized for their absence. I talked, more then I ever had, I think. I told him about my friendships and my love life. Those few girls who had preferred my skin to the wood of violins, who only liked the musical side of my job, who made fun of me because I didn't know anything about current affairs, about a book, an author or a film. Who blushed because of me in the company of others. Who turned their back on me as soon as Ireland entered the picture.

And then Tyrone Meehan spoke. There were six empty pints on the table and four more to drink. He told me about his brothers, his sisters.

—Eleven? I asked.

—Eleven, smiled Tyrone.

Two had died in infancy. The others survived. He told me their names, counting them off on his fingers. Séanna, Mary, Róisín ... He couldn't remember their ages, but he knew where they lived. Scotland, Canada, the United States, Australia, New Zealand. Apart from one sister who had become a nun and a brother who lived in Dublin, they had all chosen exile. And then Tyrone spoke of his mother. A few brief sentences told of her cowardice. And his father. Pádraig Meehan, Pat, a great Republican, a pious Catholic, a giant of a peasant, a fantastic hurler, the greatest storyteller in Killybegs, the greatest stout-drinker in Donegal, the most talented singer in the whole of Ireland. A legend of a leprechaun, a magician. And also a father who beat them. All of them, one after the other, and their mother too, every night the beer got hold of him, swearing to God that he was born too early or too late but not in the right place. Tyrone Meehan told me all this in a low voice. He called him his Bad Man. He told me he had hated him right up until his death, one windy winter morning, when he was found along the side of the road, lying in the ditch between the pub and the house, grey, his blood frozen to ice.

—Can you keep another secret? Tyrone asked me.

I said yes. He told me that no one knew about his father's blows and his hatred for him. Pat Meehan was an admirable man and that was that. He lay his hand on the table. I put mine on his. He gave his usual wink and nod. I was overwhelmed by his trust. I raised my glass. He raised his. That night, Tyrone Meehan had been betraying General Humbert for seventeen years.

They found my traitor's body on Thursday, 5 April, at three o'clock, in the living room, beside the fireplace. He was lying on his front. It was a neighbour who noticed that the door had been open since the morning. Sheila was in Belfast. So was Jack. The Gardaí said he had been killed at point-blank range by two 12-calibre buckshot bullets. The first one hit him in the groin; the second in the forehead. He had just come back from the forest. Branches were scattered around him. He was still wearing his jacket. His cap had fallen on the ground. The Gardaí found neither a note claiming responsibility, nor any trace of a struggle. The killers were waiting for him in his house. They murdered him and then left. The Gardaí on duty in cars at the crossroads noticed no suspicious vehicles. According to the preliminary results of the enquiry, the killers came to the thatched cottage by cutting through the wood.

∼

I arrived in Belfast on Sunday, 8 April, after the Easter parade. A black ribbon was tied to the front door of the house. In the living room were Jack, Sheila and some others I didn't know. The coffin was open, placed on steel trestles. Tyrone's head was bandaged. All you could see were his blue eyelids, the bridge of his nose and his thin lips. The linen cloth hid his forehead to his eyebrows, enveloping his chin and his neck. His hands were joined. I did not recognize him. I recognized nothing about him. I looked away. I touched neither the wood nor his body. There were only a few Mass cards placed on his shroud. Jack brought me a mug of tea, my mug, the one with the Eiffel tower wearing a beret. Sheila's eyes were sunken, and she wore black. She had pinned an Easter lily to her jacket. She was no longer crying. She offered me biscuits. She was coming and going, from her dead man to the little kitchen. No one came in. Jack explained that the body had been brought back from Donegal the previous night. Before that, dozens of neighbours and Republicans had come to pay their respects. Important members of Sinn Féin, leaders, volunteers of no particular rank, the head of the Belfast Brigade, two officers from the Northern Command and even one member of the IRA Army Council. As soon as the coffin arrived at the house, the visits stopped. They had come for Jack and Sheila, not for Tyrone. His friends, his comrades in arms, his ambush brothers, none of them would utter his name. They referred to him as 'that man' or 'this man'. Meehan was dead; Tyrone had never existed. The morning I arrived, the Republican movement had asked the nationalist population not to join the funeral cortege. It had also ordered its members not to take part. I told Jack that I was not concerned by this warning. While two elderly women were taking their leave, Jack pulled me into his bedroom.

—There was an internal enquiry. The IRA knows you saw Tyrone.

—What do you mean, an internal enquiry?

—You were talking in one of the pubs about having seen him.

—I didn't.

—You were drunk, Tony. Some friends came and got me so that I could get you out of there. It was me who came to get you in Burn's.

—I don't remember any of this.

—Late that afternoon, you bumped into an IRA intelligence agent without knowing it and you talked to him. He had you followed. You were going from pub to pub questioning people.

—I never said anything to anyone.

—You talked. Look, just leave it. It's not important any more.

—I did not give Tyrone's address to the IRA.

Jack shrugged his shoulders. He said that the IRA already knew where his father was. He also said that they wanted to see me. I mustn't tell them that Sheila had driven me to Donegal.

He was sitting on his bed. I was standing in front of the closed door. He had drawn the curtain. He was talking softly, smoking a cigarette. I could hear whispering from the living room. And then he looked at me. I had come with no bags. In Paris, I had put on a white shirt and my black suit. I had also bought a thin black tie. And I had come dressed like that, in this rigid fancy dress, halfway between a salesman and the Grim Reaper. Jack told me that Tyrone would be buried the next day, Monday, 9 April. He repeated the movement's warning. He assured me that my presence would be an act of courage, that I didn't have to go to the funeral. I said that this was why I was here. Jack looked relieved. I could sleep in the living room, on the sofa, beside the coffin. I said that would do just fine. Sheila went to bed around two o'clock, having kissed her husband's forehead. Jack went up to his room half an hour later. I lay down fully clothed on the blue cushions, a sheet wrapped around me.

The house was damp. It was cold. The dark unnerved me. I left the television pilot light on. The table had been pushed against the wall. The sofa and the coffin were side by side, almost touching. Twice, I half-raised myself onto my elbow, to see the white bandages and the tip of his nose. I don't think I slept. I was curled up in a ball, my forehead pressed against the cement wall. I kept seeing Tyrone's back, bent over the bundles of wood. What had I said in the pub? That I had seen Tyrone? That he had talked to me? I had no memory of it whatsoever. It seemed stupid to me. I was stupid. I should have gone back to Paris. Everyone must know that Tony the French violin-maker was one of the last to see Tyrone Meehan alive. So what? Then what? What would that change? I think I actually slept. When I opened my eyes, the first thing I saw was the wood of the coffin. I did not wash. I just splashed some water and

Wright's yellow tar soap on my face. And then I went out while we waited for the hearse to arrive.

It was arranged that the ceremony would be quick and simple. A blessing at the house, no carrying of the coffin. Jack said that Tyrone would not be buried in Miltown, in the plot where the heroes lie, but in the city cemetery, on the other side of the Falls Road. He told me that the tombstone would be engraved with his name, his date of birth and date of death and these words from the Second Epistle of St John: 'Look to yourselves'.

There were eleven of us behind the coffin. Father Byrne, an altar boy, Sheila, Jack, relations who had come from Glasgow and three small women all dressed in black. I was just behind them, standing back, head lowered. Faces peered through the windows. One woman blessed herself on her front doorstep. Young people watched us, arms folded, cigarettes in the corner of their mouths. The street was not welcoming, but not hostile either. Indifferent, rather, like when an enemy patrol passed. A line of cars followed our cortege. You don't overtake a coffin. One black taxi did. The driver beeped his horn as he was level with us, making me jump.

It was strange. For the first time in my history of Ireland, walking under her sky, I was thinking of something else. I wasn't quite there. We arrived at the iron gates of the cemetery. Walking among the graves, I could see Tyrone's strange smile again, when I asked him if he was my friend. I looked at this handful of poor people in black and grey. The coffin was lowered with straps. I stared up at the sky. I had imagined Tyrone's death oh so differently. The flag on the coffin, his gloves, his beret. Me carrying the coffin, refusing to be relieved of my load. I had imagined the military salute over his grave. Me with my arms by my sides, as I had seen volunteers do at the first notes of the national anthem.

The priest and the altar boy left by car. We walked back down the Falls, in the wind. At the house, two young girls had prepared tea and toast. We ate the toast and drank the tea. Jack pulled the table back into the middle of the living room. Sheila asked me when I was leaving.

—Tomorrow afternoon, I replied.

Jack pinned an Easter lily on my jacket. There was a do on at the Thomas Ashe. He asked me to come with him. I sat on the floor. I wasn't tired. It was as though all this had happened a long time before and Tyrone had been dead for years. He had been dead when I met him. A dead man who had taught me how to piss. He had been dead when we collected the wood. Still standing but already dead. I told myself that we had just put him to rest. That we had simply moved a cold body from life to elsewhere.

I wasn't sad for him. I wasn't sad for us. I was sad for me. Sad not to have seen, heard or felt anything. Sad about my ignorance, my affection, my certainties. I was sad for all the things I had done for him. I was sad for Sheila and Jack. And sad for Ireland, sad for my big man with his round-necked collar. Sad for the rain that had started to fall, sad for the mist on the hills, sad for the night that was descending in grey veils.

I was also angry. Angry about what he had done to us. Angry because we were here, huddled against each other with a feeling of cold disbelief in our guts, all because of him. I was angry at him for the tears he made us shed. Because he had deceived us, messed us around, broken us. I was grieving. I would now have to live with my silence and his.

In the hall of the Republican club, beyond the wire-mesh door and the surveillance cameras, a man was sitting at a table in front of a black notebook. When we came in, he got up. He shook Jack's hand, asking him if he was all right. Jack said he was. He wrote his name down and wrote mine in the visitors' column.

—So, how was the service? the Republican asked.

—A family service, Jack answered.

We went into the lounge. It was after nine o'clock. It was full. At the round table near the door, women in spring dresses were drinking rum drowned in Coke. I smiled. For a second, I saw Jim, Cathy and myself again. He, laughing louder than the rest, she, finishing other people's drinks, and I, trembling with the excitement of being there. Jack asked me to wait by the wall. He made towards the bar, apologizing, his arms stretched out to push his way through the crowd. He ordered a Guinness for me, a Harp for himself. He glanced at the tables on his way back. At the end of the room, near the stage, five men crowded around their beers. I knew one of them: Mike O'Doyle. Tyrone had introduced us one Easter Sunday, at the beginning of my Irish voyage. O'Doyle saw us. He raised his hand. Jack responded. O'Doyle beckoned us over. Jack hesitated. I saw him bite his lip. He looked at me. He seemed anxious. He asked me to follow him anyway. As we approached, O'Doyle spoke briefly to two of the men drinking with him. They took their beers and went to sit at another table. Mike stood up. He shook Jack's hand and took mine.

—We've met, Tony, said Mike O'Doyle, smiling.

I nodded. He had me sit down, between a guy with a broken nose and a very thin man with a scarred face. Jack was not at ease. He was talking to the ex-prisoner with the broken nose. I stared at my beer and all the wet circles staining the table.

—We're really sorry about your da, O'Doyle said.

Jack raised his eyes to heaven.

'We had nothing to do with the death of Mr Meehan,' the IRA had stated on the day of Tyrone's murder.

—How's Sheila?

—It hasn't really sunk in yet.

—And what about you? Will you be ok?

—We're going to have to sell the house.

Mike O'Doyle looked thoughtful. The two other guys said nothing.

—Who could have done it? I asked.

O'Doyle looked at me, smiling. He shrugged and took a swig of beer.

—Anyone can shoot a hunting bullet into an unarmed man.

—Who is anyone?

—Tony! Jack whispered.

—Leave it, Meehan. He's right to ask, answered O'Doyle.

The Republican kept looking at me. I didn't lower my eyes. He glanced at his two friends, at the crowd dancing to disco music. He asked Broken Nose to get some more beers. He spoke in a low voice.

—Anyone, Tony. Anyone means from the Brits to Loyalist paramilitaries, from dissident Republicans to the sons of any of his victims, along with the local farmer who saw Tyrone on his way and who gave himself courage with a few pints before emptying his rifle. That's anyone, Tony.

—And the IRA?

—Mike has answered that question, Tony.

—I've answered that question, Tony.

—What about an IRA man, operating on his own, for revenge?

—The IRA is an army, Tony. There is no man operating on his own.

—Well, who then?

—Why not you, Tony? For pride, for revenge too. Along with Sheila, you were the only one to visit him. So you see, why not you?

—Because it wasn't me.

—There you go: 'because'. That's the right answer. And it wasn't the IRA because it wasn't the IRA. The person who killed Tyrone Meehan was called Tyrone Meehan.

The table filled with fresh pints. Mike O'Doyle put his arm on Jack Meehan's shoulder and drew him down to talk. Jack nodded his head several times. Then he thanked him, clasping his hand. When he lifted his head, he seemed appeased. He breathed in deeply and picked up his pint.

—Sláinte!

The others responded, raising their glasses.

—Slan'cheh, I murmured like them.

I carefully sipped the creamy head. I drank slowly, letting the bitterness take over. I closed my eyes. On the stage the DJ was playing seventies' classics. I asked Jack if he wanted another beer. He still had two lined up. Mike refused as well, with a wave of his hand. He looked at me. He leaned towards me and told me to follow him. I looked up at Jack. He nodded. So I stood up.

We went to the toilets. Mike O'Doyle went in first. The large room was full of men talking. This was the place to go if you wanted some peace and quiet. He steered me gently towards the far wall, beneath the barred window. He turned his back to the room and I faced him, leaning against the tiling. He crossed his arms and tilted his head. He looked at me without saying a word. He was waiting for something. I didn't know what. Behind us, men were pissing, laughing, slapping each other on the back. We were still and silent.

—He didn't tell me anything, I murmured.

—And?

—And nothing. He didn't tell me anything.

—I know he didn't tell you anything. And now what?

—I don't understand. You're talking too fast.

—We had advised you not to go.

—But I wanted to know.

—Know what?

—To know if there were things that were true during all that time.

—Things?

—Feelings, like friendship.

Mike O'Doyle nodded. He put his hands in his pockets. He looked bemused.

—Friendship, he repeated.

Then he turned around. He crossed the room and took a piss.

—Does the beer not do this to you?

I said it did and went over beside him.

—When are you leaving?

—Tomorrow.

—We'll have to find a bed for you if Sheila sells the house.

I turned my head. O'Doyle staring at the ceiling, doing up his trousers. He said he would introduce me to a woman who lived in Ballymurphy. Winking, he told me that he knew her very well. An old Republican lady. She was adorable, her door always open for the boys, the tea always scalding. During the war she would add small gifts to the prisoners' packages, and wrote letters to the more isolated ones. She had marched her whole life, O'Doyle told me. She never lowered her eyes in front of an Englishman. She never complained about anything. She had a room upstairs that she sometimes lent to friends. I could stay there, for now.

We were about to leave the toilets. Before pushing the swinging door, Mike turned around. I tried to read his face.

—It's the Brits we want to drive out of here, not violin-makers.

I smiled at him. He looked at the hall. He searched all around until he noticed a table of women near the door.

—Come here a second, he said.

I followed him. The crowd was happy. I felt nauseous, overwhelmed by the burial and the beer. I tripped. Mike caught me just before I hit the ground. A man laughed, saying something I didn't understand. When we reached the table, Mike O'Doyle crouched down beside an old woman who took his hands. She was drinking vodka. Her friends were around her, speaking quickly and loudly. I remained standing. I bent down. Mike introduced me. As a Frenchman, a violin-maker and a friend of Tyrone Meehan.

—May God have mercy on his soul, murmured the woman, lifting her eyes towards me.

Behind her glasses, her eyes were like an eagle's, steel and sky. Her sharp face was lined with wrinkles. She wore an ivory blouse and a blue skirt. She was small and slight. She kept saying 'Paris' like a magic word. She laughed saying 'Charles de Gaulle', French style, and also 'Oh là là' like Maurice Chevalier.

Her name was Gráinne O'Doyle. She was seventy-eight years old. Her son Mike told her my story. The other women listened, leaning forward. He said that if Sheila Meehan sold her house, I would have to go to a hotel, so I may as well take the upstairs bedroom. Gráinne laughed again. She replied that I would be good company for her since she could no longer count on her son to switch off the television when she fell asleep. Mike protested. She ran her fingers through his hair, laughing. Then he stood up. He pushed me towards her before going back to our table.

In turn, I crouched down in front of the old woman, my hands in hers. She said OK. That it would make her happy, that it was impossible to leave a violin-maker out on the street. And French at that! She said I'd have to tell her about my job, and Paris, and my love life. Her drinking buddies shouted in agreement. 'Especially his love life!' said one of them, a large lady with her hair in a tight white bun. Gráinne laughed. She said she would tell me about

Seán, her husband, who died ten years ago, tortured and then killed by a vicious cancer. About Mike, her son, a good man, but a child too, who gave her sleepless nights and made her blood run cold. She said this, stroking my thumbs with the silk of her own, her eyes filled with tears. A Claddagh ring shone on her finger. I missed mine. I would find it; I would put it back on. I would also look for my soft cap, abandoned in a corner of my workshop.

Gráinne moved closer. She said she would tell me about Ireland. Everything I thought I knew, but didn't. She said that she would also tell me about Tyrone Meehan, the good-looking lad he was when he was twenty. She leaned forward. It felt like we were alone. She sitting, me kneeling on the ground. She spoke in a low voice. Her face was familiar to me. For a second I thought of Mise Éire. But that wasn't it. She was even more beautiful, more lively and more sorrowful. She said that she had seen me that morning, at the funeral. She had been there, in the cortège, with her two sisters. The three shadows of grief who had walked in front of me. She told me she had done it for Sheila. For Tyrone, she went to the chapel and lit two candles. One for the bad that he had done, the other for him to be forgiven. My head was heavy, my right knee in pain. Her skin brushed against mine.

—Just because that old eejit double-crossed us doesn't mean you should forget about us, whispered Gráinne, smiling.

I don't know why she said that. She said that there were Tyrones everywhere, in wartime and in peace, and that it didn't change anything, neither about the war nor about peace. Nor even about Tyrone. She said that we had loved him without holding back because he was who he was. And that we had given him our trust because he was him.

I nodded. I smiled. I could picture us again. The way we pulled up the collars of our raincoats. Me, following in his footsteps. His expression beneath his cap. Our glasses raised. His hand. I looked at the hall. I let a tear form.

Gráinne told me that I was welcome to stay with her next time. That I shouldn't think twice about it. That I should just knock on her door. The only condition was that I would accompany her to Mass on Sunday mornings. And also – she was no longer laughing – that I would bring her a bottle of cognac, the real stuff, with the word France written in gold on the label.

Why *My Traitor*?

[ORIGINALLY PUBLISHED AS A SEPARATE COMMENTARY]

I have rarely written about Ireland apart from in a newspaper. I had promised myself that. I had spent so much time telling the story of the war in the north of this country that the conflict would always be a news zone for me. Reports, inquiries, analysis, getting people to see, hear, understand. That was all. And it was a choice.

This war was cruel and dirty, a war in the shadows, which had to be put into words. As a journalist with *Libération* I gave a balanced account of each side's hopes. As a human, my heart went out to the Republicans.

Over the last thirty years I've often been asked why I didn't write anything else about Northern Ireland. Write. That meant going beyond the newspaper interviews. People asked me about the possibility of a book. A document, an essay, an account, a novel. And I said no. Every time. Whatever was worth publishing had been on a daily basis, in a daily paper. It was for the Irish material, in particular, that I had received the Albert Londres Prize in

1988. It seemed to me that this work couldn't receive any higher recognition.

That's where I was at on Christmas Eve, 2005.

And then the news came that there was a traitor to the Republican struggle. For those who love the brutality of names, he was called Denis Donaldson. It was 'Denis' before his betrayal, then 'Donaldson' afterwards. Some people even referred to him as 'that man'. No more first name, no more surname. That man, and that was all. Denis was Catholic, funny, attentive, dazzling. Denis was a friend. He was one of those whom I introduced to passing journalists to convince them that commitment to the cause could sometimes rhyme with elegance. Denis had been an IRA soldier. He had held an important position at the heart of Sinn Féin. He was in on all the speeches, all the demonstrations. He suffered like the others and he dreamed like the others. Ireland was his battle. He drank, he sang, he hugged you, he took your arm to tell you a secret. He was committed to the cause forever, and nothing ever betrayed him. He was the one above suspicion. That's him there in the photo at the Long Kesh prisoners' camp, with his arm around the shoulders of Bobby Sands, the patriot who died on hunger strike, a martyr and a worldwide symbol of the Irish conflict.

Denis Donaldson. Good soldier, good husband, good friend. An honest expression in his eyes, a firm handshake, a magnificent smile. A traitor. Their traitor. And my traitor too.

In December 2005, Denis was unmasked. He confessed because the noose was tightening around him after the peace process. He confessed because his situation had become untenable. I was in an airport when I heard about it; a phone call on my mobile just before I turned it off to go through customs. I understood for the first time what it means to collapse. The dizziness, the sudden pain, the trembling hands, the weak knees, the tears.

Denis. Our Denis. He had been a traitor for almost twenty years. His beloved Ireland, his struggle, his parents, his children, his comrades, his friends, me. He had betrayed us. Every morning, every evening. For a few thousand pounds sterling he had been an informer for the British army, the secret services, the Northern Irish police. He drank in the pubs, he sang in the pubs, he spied in the pubs. He spied, especially. He was in the thick of everything. At the heart of Sinn Féin, at the heart of the Northern Irish parliament, at the heart of the peace negotiations and in all our hearts.

He gave himself up to his comrades in arms, head lowered and eyes defeated. He was interrogated for a long time by the IRA. He refused to explain his betrayal. He was released. And he decided to stay at home, in Ireland. To leave Belfast for the other side of the border, a rural cottage in Donegal. Despite the comfort of his devastated family, he was isolated. He was condemned. He waited.

There was great disarray in the community. Each did what he could. For a rare few, Denis stayed Denis. For others he became Donaldson. Or 'that man'. Or unmentionable. Some tried to understand, others to forget.

Me, I wrote. I decided that it was now or never, both painful and possible. I wrote. I needed to. But I didn't work like a journalist. No reporting on Denis, no inquiry into Denis, nothing like that. I decided to go around him, to forget the expression in his eyes, to forget his name. I distanced myself from him, from myself, from ourselves, in order to observe better.

So here is *My Traitor*.

The story of Antoine, a Parisian violin-maker who discovers Ireland's music. He knows nothing about the North. It doesn't matter to him. His heroes are bow-makers, the great violin-makers of legend. War hasn't touched him yet. This is Antoine. Who will become Tony for those in Belfast. Because he will see them live, and suffer and fight. And because in return they will love him like a son.

And then there is Tyrone Meehan. Ireland is his battle. He drinks, he sings, he hugs you, he takes your arm to tell you a secret. He is committed to the cause forever and nothing could ever betray him. He is the one above suspicion. This is Tyrone, his friend, his brother, his own traitor.

Tyrone is not Denis. But the look in their eyes is the same. I am not Antoine. But our pain is the same.

When I started writing this, Denis was alive. I secretly dreamt of seeing him again, face to face, to ask him if our friendship was real. Just that. To know, about us. It was a childish question, both stupid and vain, but that's the way it was. 'I compromised myself during a vulnerable time in my life.' That's what he admitted to his comrades. That's all he would say. And all we will know.

Denis Donaldson was executed on 4 April 2006, while I was writing the story of Tyrone Meehan. Killed with a hunting weapon in the small family cottage where he was hiding. I never saw him again. He never answered my question. So I asked Antoine to do that for me. To cross the border. To see Tyrone, his friend, his traitor, just before he dies. To knock on his door and go in. He did that. They met face to face in a damp cottage. They sat on either side of a small table, a piping hot cup of tea in their hands. There was a fire in the hearth. It was dark. They talked. And I was there. I was there.